SIREN

OF

SONG

IMMORTAL WORLD

BOOK TWO

<u>TRIGGER WARNING</u>

This book contains sensitive material relating to:

Child abuse

Sexual Assault

Murder

Crude language

Slavery

Sexism

Bigotry

Homophobia

Violence

Sex

Substance Abuse

Hunting

Illegal Activities

Destruction

Genocide

*Please note the spice level is low in this book.

I would like to dedicate this book to all the survivors out there

and to my friends and family who have stood by me and supported me

not just through this creative process, but through my own darkness.

Immortal World

Book 2: SIREN OF SONG

Prolog

Twelve thousand or so years ago

Kassie…

Much to our mother's dismay, our first, second, and even third
cycles had come and gone without our powers developing. She had told
us that we had to grow into them but for some reason, they were not
appearing. She had said that because we were half siren and half deity,
perhaps our reaching womanhood the first time wasn't enough but that
it would happen with our next cycle.

When our powers, or any for that matter, continued to fail to
appear in the next year, Mother and our aunts lured a tremendous

wooden ship without completely entrancing the crew. They had hidden from view and told us to stand where we could be seen. In our fourteen years, we'd never seen males up close, constantly being made to watch from a distance. When the males got off the ship and approached us it wasn't as we'd expected. They didn't come to us in admiration, seeking to fulfill our every desire; they came with weapons drawn as they circled us. This moment was my first taste of fear.

We were then forced onto the ship. Aella put up the biggest fight. Amaltheia was trying to plead with them, and I called out for our mother. I could see her there, hidden from sight on a hibiscus-covered hill. One of our aunts rested a hand on her shoulder as if to restrain her should she try to come for us; she never did. The hot tears that had streamed down my face were the first I'd cried in fear instead of pain. Did my mother know fear? I'd heard her and our aunts talking about how we couldn't stay if we had no powers, but was this intended to bring forth our powers, or was our future to be uncertain?

Despite our struggles, we were dragged onto the ship quickly and restrained. By the time we reached dry land, the males had locked us in a strange metal cage with straw in the bottom. Amaltheia had told them that we were sirens and that they would suffer when we came into our powers. Most of the males aboard the ship had backed away from us, but one had laughed and told her she was an ignorant girl.

Our dank, rocking, and swaying journey had thankfully lasted only a handful of days before they hauled us off the ship. As they carried us in the cage to our destination, I looked out at the towering stone walls and the crowds of people. I'd never seen so many people, not even if I'd tallied all the males our mother and aunts had lured to our island. Children were roaming about; most seemed dressed in filthy clothing and paid no attention to us. It wasn't long after that when my sisters and I were separated for nearly ten years.

The queen had taken me as her personal slave. She'd seemed kind enough, yet there was something almost terrifying about her just beneath the surface. When I'd asked where my sisters had been sent to, she looked at me with pity and told me I'd have to be punished if I asked questions above my station again. She'd taught me with apologies and whippings to my back, but never hard enough to break the skin. She'd said she didn't want to hurt me, only to teach me my place. I only hoped my sisters were treated better.

Chapter 1

Kassie…

"All right, Kassie, it's your turn to sing while we get the coypu," Ella said as we trudged through the bayou, mud boots up to our knees, wearing old jeans, tank tops, and carrying machetes and a rifle in case of gators. The fact that water-dwelling critters weakened us had always pissed me off.

"Goodie," I said with little enthusiasm. I hated being the bait when it was much more fun to be the one with the machete.

"What are you complaining about? I'm the one with the stupid gun. As if we need it, those stupid gators couldn't kill us if they wanted to," Theia complained.

"You don't know that, Theia; what if we find a bunch of them, and they overpower us? Then they could eat us, and we would die because, eventually, our heads would be separated from our bodies. How do you kill an immortal?" Ella asked.

We both rolled our eyes, but Theia answered, "Sever the head from the body. I know, I know."

"Good, then shut up so Sandy can start singing," Ella said in a voice that anyone other than her sisters would have called bland.

"I hate it when you call me that," I muttered. Theia blew me a kiss from her middle finger, earning a glare from me as I started singing. Anything worked on the creatures. Our voices mesmerized them, and unfortunately, every other critter in these parts. Coypu were ugly little swamp rats, but they tasted good and soothed a siren's throat.

"There's one!" Theia said in an excited whisper. Ella nodded, and they circled to either side of me, closing in on the large rodent. Suddenly, birds flew from the trees, the Coypu darted away, and I could hear a crashing sound tearing through the swamp toward us.

"What the hell?" Ella straightened, holding her machete at the ready.

I stopped singing and pulled out my machete as Theia lifted the pump action shotgun. "That's not a gator." I took a step back, looking in the direction of the noise.

"Could it be a bear?' Theia asked as she and Ella backed toward me. We may be immortal, but that didn't mean we would just let whatever was coming at us attack without a defense. After all, we were the daughters of the Greek god of war.

"Sounds bigger," Ella said.

A roar like nothing I'd ever heard sounded off in the distance, the crashing sound coming closer. "Should we run or something?" I asked, unsure if just standing at the ready was the best idea.

"The only things in this swamp we can't charm are water-dwelling critters; we just need to be sure this thing's close enough to hear us," Theia replied confidently.

"And anything without a heartbeat," Ella added, always chock-full of survival need-to-knows.

"I don't think it's a fuckin Zombie or Vamp, Ella!" Theia snapped.

My eyes widened as the massive creature came into view in the distance. "It's fucking Bigfoot!"

"Do our songs work on those things?" Theia asked in horror as she raised the shotgun.

"You know as much as I do about those apes!" Ella yelled, pissed off.

I glanced at my sisters and then back at Bigfoot before saying, "One way to find out." I began to sing again, my sisters joining in. The creature skidded to a halt, looking at the three of us and breathing heavily. He shook his head, sniffed the air, and let out another roar before turning and disappearing into the thick swamp with almost no effort. I breathed a sigh of relief. "Maybe he was just after something."

"Yeah, well, he disturbed my dinner," Theia growled. "I should have just shot him."

"We don't even know if Bigfoot can be killed," Ella said calmly before continuing, "if he's an immortal, then you would have only succeeded in pissing him off."

"And when he got close enough, you would have hacked his head off without flinching," I said, knowing our sister all too well. Ella was cold, calculated, and lived to shed blood in battle. Out of the three of us, she was the most like our father.

"What would you have done? Kept him as a pet?" Theia teased with a wink.

I rolled my eyes. "Can we find something else for dinner if we're not going to have coypu?"

"Who says we're not?" Ella asked as she threw the machete. It hit with a wet crunch and a squeak that lasted only seconds.

"I'm not cleaning that," I said, still a bit pissed about being bait. We all walked over to the kill, disappointed that it was an opossum, bagged it, and began heading back to the plantation house.

Ella stopped and turned to look into the trees. "Be ready for a fight," she said in a low voice.

"What is it?" I asked, trying to see what she was seeing.

"Is Bigfoot still stalking us?" Theia asked.

Ella began walking again, getting about three feet ahead of us. "Yes."

"Do you think he's going to attack?" I asked, feeling slightly nervous because I knew nothing about the creature.

"I think he's just making sure we leave his swamp," Ella told me. "But I could be wrong."

"Gee, thanks," my voice dripped with sarcasm.

"Tomorrow, I need you to go into town and hire a guide to take us deeper into the swamp, into territory that hopefully doesn't belong to Bigfoot," Ella said bitterly.

"If you think it's necessary." I agreed without complaint. Of the three of us, I was the best at dealing with humans and, by far, the best at coping with males of any kind. As sirens, we could get a male to do whatever we wanted them to. As individuals, we each had our reasons for hating human interaction. It had always been up to me to find the most agreeable human without the need of our powers.

Ella stopped off at our processing station to clean the opossum while I took the weapons inside to clean them up. If she was asking me to go into town then I knew her itch must be getting bad. My own itch had me seeking relief nearly every night. I hated the never-ending lust that came with being a siren. Not that I didn't like sex, it was the fact that self-satisfaction was nearly impossible to obtain. Eventually, we would need to seek out lovers to relieve the ache. No matter how much I pumped my fingers in and out of my body, no matter the toys used, satisfaction was always easier to find release with another body.

The next day, I got up and left our rundown plantation home, heading into town. The sound of cicadas filled my ears as I drove down the old dirt road. Keeping a low profile was a way of life for us, so actively seeking a guide to unknown parts of the bayou had me on edge as I parked our beaten-up old green Dodge. I could feel everyone's eyes on me as I walked down the sidewalks toward the docks. We'd chosen a small town so there would be less chance of our songs being heard, but unfortunately, that meant people would notice us. I wanted nothing more than to turn around and head back to the plantation home, but instead, I held my head high and continued toward the docks.

Taking a deep breath, I stepped into the light bustle of the docks. A young male with dark hair immediately smiled and approached me. "What's a pretty thing like you doing in a place like this?" His cheesy pickup line flowed smoothly off his tongue, a line he'd no doubt used before.

"She's probably looking for someone who doesn't make her skin crawl." Another voice said from off to the side before I could say anything to the guy flirting with me.

"So not you," he said as he glared at the second man.

I turned to the second man, anticipating his response to be another cheap line intended to woo me. "Probably not. I smell like the swamp, but at least I can tell when a woman's not interested in pickup lines." He smiled as he walked up. "Name's Clay Higgons. If you're looking for the boss, he ain't coming in today."

I gave him a quick once over, taking in his mud boots, jeans, and sleeveless shirt. "Who goes the deepest into the bayou?"

"Fuck," said the first man, drawing my attention for only a moment.

Clay smiled. "That would be me, and Jack here knows it."

"Are you for hirer?" I asked, not looking at Jack any longer.

"Don't you wanna see my boat?" Clay asked with a smile, his amber eyes twinkling with amusement.

"If it gets deeper in the bayou than anyone else's and can hold my two sisters and myself, I don't care what it looks like," I informed him in a bland tone.

He glanced at Jack, who was walking away. "I'd ask what you and your sisters are looking for out there, but as long as I'm paid and I get to irritate that idiot, I don't care."

"We will pay you in cash, half when we get on the boat, the other half when the trip is over," I told him, glancing around to be sure no one was close enough to hear what I was saying.

He chewed the inside of his lip for a moment before nodding. "Sounds fair enough."

"There are a few conditions," I warned, getting to the part I didn't like.

"Like I said, I get paid; I'm happy," he reiterated, his tall, broad frame relaxed.

"My sisters and I don't do well around people; in fact, unless they talk to you, don't talk to them, agreed?"

"Unless necessary, you'll be the only one I talk to; after all, you're the one I'm doing business with," he loosely agreed.

I narrowed my eyes. "Next, we have the right to refuse to answer any questions you have."

"The less I know, the more deniability I have; it has always been my motto," he replied, never breaking eye contact.

"You will be the only other person on the boat, no animals, either." The risk of just one person hearing our siren's call was more than enough; there was no way I was going to worry about a dog or another human.

"Do I tell you my fee now or later," he asked with a half smile.

"I'm sure we can afford whatever you charge," I told him, relieved that he had not questioned any of my requirements.

"I have one favor to ask you, well, two," he said with a wink.

I narrowed my eyes. "You don't even know my name, and you're asking for favors?"

"First, tell me your name; second, act like Jack is invisible every time you see him," he said, still smiling.

I felt the corner of my mouth turn up in amusement. "You drive a hard bargain, Mr. Higgons. You may call me Kassie."

"Mr. Higgons is a bit old sounding for my taste. Why don't we just go with Clay? After all, you've only given me your first name, and if I were to call you by your last name, then your sisters might think I'm addressing them."

"I'll see you tomorrow morning at this address, 7:00 a.m.," I said, handing him a slip of paper with the plantation's abandoned dock number. I hadn't given him a last name because we didn't have them. We were born before they existed.

"And the shady dealings continue," he mocked before confirming, "tomorrow morning." Without another word, I turned and headed home. Tomorrow would tell if this had been too easy or if good fortune had indeed smiled on me for a change. Clay Higgons seemed to be uninterested in anything but a job, and that was exactly what we needed, although the itch in my throat told me I would soon need something else.

Being a siren wasn't easy. Most immortal races hated or feared us because of our power to entrap males. Some even hunted us. They didn't know that our powers enslaved us as well. No matter how badly any of us want to deny our songs, the urge to have our needs satisfied would force our songs from us. Ella was the only one of the three of us to succeed in denying her song for centuries. The last time she lost that fight was the fall of Troy in a fit of jealousy after Aphrodite took Helen from her. The humans believed the kings were obsessed with Helen when in reality, it was my sister. Ella used her Siren's Call on the males to destroy Troy when Helen had betrayed her. Not to mention the role our father had played in it all.

As I walked into our home, Theia paused her game and pushed her headset off one ear. "Did you get it taken care of?"

"His name is Clay Higgons, and he'll be at the dock at 7:00 a.m.," I told her as I walked over, picked up my book from the coffee table, and sat next to her. "He seems like he's only interested in getting paid, and he didn't even question any of the rules I gave him."

"That's good," Theia said as she pushed her headset back in place.

I lifted it off her ear again. "Where is Ella?"

"In the barn with her best friend, where else?" Theia asked, then unpaused her game and fixed her headset with a pointed look.

With a sigh, I put down my book and got up. Ella was pissed; she'd gone to bed pissed. It wasn't like any of us were happy with the situation. I walked out to the barn, where the bap-bap-bap of her punches filled the space. The chains rattled on the punching bag, and the rafters squeaked as the bag jostled with each assault. "You going to stay out here all day?" I asked.

"I might go find a gator to wrestle later," Ella said blandly.

"Ella." I clicked my tongue. Others might think she was joking, but Theia and I knew just how unhinged our sister could occasionally get.

"Relax. I'm joking," she said as she caught the bag, and stopped its swing. "Did you find someone?"

Swallowing, I walked over to the weights. "Yeah, no women working at the docks again."

"Of fucking course not! Why the fuck would the fates smile on us for a damn change? What's this asshole like? Did he use any sleazy pickup lines?" She snarled the question, anger being one of her only emotions.

"Actually, he seems like he's just in it for the money. In fact, he told the other jerk there that he could tell when a woman wasn't interested. I liked how professional he was. He didn't ask any questions or argue any of the rules I gave him, either."

"Sounds like a sneak to me," she said bitterly.

I sighed. "Maybe, but do we really have any choice?"

"Unless you feel like sparring with me, you need to go cram your nose in a book or plant some flowers or something," Ella said, effectively dismissing me. Out of the three of us, Ella was the most violent. Her years leading up to immortality had left her with a more toned appearance than Theia and I. She was a beautiful, cold warrior, her short, darker hair pulled back in a ponytail.

Setting my shoulders, I decided to take her up on her offer. "Not a fight, just some sparring?"

Ella turned to me and gave a ghost of a smile, her blue-gray eyes twinkling. "Think you can handle it, Sandy?"

Narrowing my eyes, I changed my stance. "Bring it, Ells," I said, using her hated nickname. With that, the punching, kicking, dodging, and flipping began. All three of us had mastered nearly every fighting style ever made, and we practiced with each other without fear of landing a solid strike. By the time we were finished, the two of us were out of breath, covered in sweat and grime, and bleeding in a few places. Ella had pinned me face down on the dirt floor of the barn before I'd given up. She had always been the strongest, and it was rare for Theia or I to win against her.

We walked into the house together, and Theia pushed her headset back. "Everything okay?"

"Just sparring," I replied.

"Did you win this time?" Theia's rich brown eyes twinkled with excitement.

I smiled and rolled my eyes. "No, I wasn't angry enough to even come close against Ella."

"You just need to practice more," Ella said as she headed up the stairs to her room and shower.

Theia shook her head. "Ella lives in two states of being."

"I know, pissed off or stone cold." I pulled my shirt over my head and wiped the sweat and grime from my face. "She's headed into pissed, I figured she needed a little outlet before she meets Clay tomorrow, or we'll be out a boatman."

"Clay? Why not Mr. Higgons?" Theia asked, twisting around, sitting her petite frame cross-legged on the couch, and latching onto the informality of using his first name.

I rolled my eyes. "He said Mr. Higgons made him feel old and to call him Clay. Plus, it makes it easier for me to think of him as a golem."

She laughed, her nose ring glinting in the light of her game. "I'll have to remember that when I meet him tomorrow. You did tell him not to talk to us, right?"

"Yes, he said unless necessary, I'm the one he's doing business with, so it shouldn't be a problem."

"Good, go shower now because you look like shit and smell like B.O." Theia turned back to her game and put her headset back in place.

With a glare, I threw my shirt at her and went to my room, still able to hear her laughter as I closed the door. The sparring with Ella had helped take a little of my frustration away, but not enough. I turned on my shower, stripped, and stepped under the spray. The irritation in my throat was still there. It was only a matter of time before I wouldn't be able to deny it any longer. The three of us would all be feeling the itch soon. At least I knew a male who came off as a womanizer now, so there was always that option, but I would put it off as long as I could.

I got out of the shower and wiped the steam from the mirror. I ran a comb through my long blond hair and tossed it into a loose braid to sleep, knowing it would be easier to manage in the morning. Looking at myself, I took in my bright blue eyes and soft features. My gently rounded face and wide eyes made me look delicate, innocent even, but I wasn't innocent— none of us were.

<u>Chapter 2</u>

Kassie…

Five o'clock in the morning beeped. Sighing, I rolled over and tapped the dismiss on my phone. Getting out of bed, I walked into the kitchen and poured myself a cup of coffee. I could hear Theia moving upstairs, so I poured her a cup as well, adding sugar and milk to hers, and only milk to mine. I walked back into the living room and over to the bottom of the steps, waiting to hand her the cup.

She came bouncing down the steps, tossing her long, highlighted hair into a quick bun as she did so. "Thanks, Kassie," she said with a smile as she took the cup I offered.

"You know I can braid your hair back for a better hold," I told her, eyeing the messy, lopsided bun on top of her head.

"You know, you look real cute in those pink shorts and your little lacy top," she said with a wink, ignoring my comment on her hair.

I rolled my eyes. "Let's go outside with Ella and see if she's ready for a refill." Theia was wearing boy shorts and a tank top, exposing the tattoos across her chest, arms, and legs.

"Oh, you mean her cup of black bitterness that matches her soul? Sure, why not?" Theia shrugged and picked up the pot of coffee as I opened the door for us to walk out to the front porch.

Ella sat on the steps, machete on her lap, running the sharpening stone over the blade with precision and care. "I hope you brought more coffee."

"Bitter and black, just like your personality," Theia said cheerfully.

"Theia, do you have to start before the sun is even up?" I asked, sitting down beside an emotionless Ella.

"She knows I love her, right bitch?" Theia asked with a wink as she topped off Ella's cup.

"Kiss-kiss hoe," Ella said in her bland morning tone.

"Told you." Theia chirped happily before bouncing back inside to put the coffee pot back on the brewer causing me to roll my eyes.

I leaned against one of the pillars, closing my eyes and listening to the rhythmic sound of Ella sharpening the blade mingled with the calls of the swamp birds. So many immortals hated us simply for what we were and for what we couldn't change, but they didn't know that we were no different than the rest of them. My sisters and I were just surviving. Theia had her online gaming, Ella had her weapons and training routines, and I had my books where I would escape into a world of fantasy. Theia and I would sing, dance, laugh, and drink now and then. Ella would get a light of excitement in her eyes when we would spar or talk about the newest weaponry available. The three of us would watch women's cage fighting and wrestling together. We didn't live to entrap men; we lived for each other and to kill Ares.

"You're not going back to sleep over there, are you Kass-Kass?" Theia asked as she came back out and sat beside me.

I smiled at her. "Nope, just listening to the birds sing without being hated for it."

Theia rolled her eyes, and Ella stopped sharpening to look at me. "If you want to sing without being judged, then you can bring dinner in today," Ella said, intending to comfort me and failing.

"Look, we are what we are. It doesn't matter if we use our powers when we sing or not; haters are gonna hate," Theia said.

"I hate how perky you are in the mornings," Ella said to Theia.

She winked at Ella. "I can't help it if I get up excited to pester you."

Ella took a drink of her coffee while holding eye contact with Theia, then calmly returned to sharpening the machete. I shook my head. "Eventually, you're going to sharpen the blade down to nothing, you know that, right?"

"Then I can get the new one I've been looking at," Ella said with an edge of excitement in her voice, which only Theia and I would pick up on.

"It's good to know that there is something that gets you excited in the morning, even if it is weapons," Theia said before taking a drink of her coffee.

"Ella, do you want me to go get my hair stuff and braid your hair back nice and tight?" I asked, drawing the conversation away from Theia's teasing.

"Sure," Ella said without looking at me. Sighing, I got up and went in to get my things. I came back out and sat down behind Ella, who had stopped sharpening the machete. "Nothing fancy or I'll kick your ass," she said as she sat there, staring at the grandfather moss hanging from the trees that surrounded our property.

"I get it, practical and tactical," I assured her, then set to work. It wasn't long before I'd braided her hair, and the three of us had finished our coffee. We went inside and fixed our breakfast of eggs, grits, bacon, and toast. After breakfast, Ella took over cleaning up while Theia and I went to our rooms to get dressed. By 6:45, we were pulling on our mud boots and walking to the boat dock with our hunting gear.

To my surprise, Clay was already waiting for us when we reached the dock. He nodded in greeting. "Morning, Miss Kassie. I hope you don't mind my being early. I wanted to be sure to find the place in time."

"Not at all. These are my sisters, Theia and Ella. We want to go deeper into the bayou to hunt some game. If you know of any good hunting areas well away from others, that would be ideal," I informed him as Theia and Ella got on the boat.

"I might know a place. I'm sure I don't need to tell you that it's dangerous out there," he said, looking at the shotgun I was packing.

"We can manage," Theia said in a tight voice.

"Legalities, I have to say it," Clay said with a shrug. "What y'all get into is your own business, so long as I get paid."

"You're right; he's not a total scum ball," Theia said to me and I felt myself turn red as Clay chuckled.

We rode in silence for forty-five minutes before we stopped. "There should be all kinds of game in this area, and no one comes to these parts, so no worries that you'll accidentally shoot anyone. If you need any help with bringing anything back, I'll be here." Clay said as he settled back in his seat and pulled out a tattered book.

We got off the fan boat and trudged into the swamp. Birds called, and frogs croaked as our boots squished and sucked in and out of the slimy mud and murky puddles. Mosquitoes and other insects buzzed about, ignoring our existence as we went deeper into the swamp and further from Clay. We spent the next few hours hunting for enough meat to last us a few days before heading back to the fan boat, giving up on finding any coypu for the day.

When we returned to the boat, Clay stood up and held out his hand. "Need me to take some of those critters for you?"

"We don't need your help," Ella said in a bitter tone.

He held up his hands. "You're the boss."

"Thanks, but we got it," I said, shooting a glare at Ella, who didn't seem to care. "What were you reading while we were out there?" I asked, knowing I was only a few chapters away from finishing my current book.

"It's a fantasy book. Gets me out of the swamp without costing me an arm and a leg," he said with a smile.

I smiled back at him as I sat down. "I can understand that. Fantasy is actually my favorite type of book to read."

"You don't say? Maybe we can swap books sometime, assuming you haven't already read this one." Clay handed the book to me as he started up the boat. After reading the title, I realized that he was reading the same book as I was and laughed. "What?" He asked over the noise of the boat.

"I'm only a few chapters away from finishing this one now."

"If you look, I think I have about five chapters left to go. You got any good books to recommend as my next read? Sitting on this boat while others go off and do whatever can get a little boring," he shouted over the fan.

I thought for a moment before making my recommendations. We made the rest of the trip back in silence. "See you back here in two days at the same time?" I asked Clay.

"Sure thing. Stay out of trouble, Kassie, unless it's in a book, in which case get right in the middle of that mess," he said with a smile.

I smiled back at him. "That's the best kind of trouble." Theia and Ella pushed past me and onto the dock. "See you," I said, grabbing my things and following my sisters.

"You don't have to make conversation with the boatman unless you want to," Theia said as I caught up with them.

"I was honestly interested in his book. The two of you don't read as much as I do, so I thought I'd ask," I said, feeling embarrassed and defensive.

"Yeah, I get that. Ella may not, but she can get over it." Theia assured me.

"I just don't want the male getting any ideas," Ella said in a bitter tone. Her hatred of males was one of the only times she showed any real emotion.

"I asked him about a book, Ella. He hardly even looked at you or Theia, and the only time he looked at me was to talk to me. For all we know, he could be into males." I tried to soothe Ella before her bitterness led to a fight with one of us.

"He's not gay, trust me, I know gay," Ella said, the blandness back in her voice. She would know if he was gay. A millennia of being with only females had given her an exceptional gaydar.

"He still didn't hardly pay any attention to either of you," I muttered as we cleaned the small game we'd gotten.

Theia sighed heavily as she tossed a hide in the scrap bucket. "I still want a coypu. I know the things are endangered, but something about them helps with the damn itch!"

"My throat started yesterday," I admitted. We hunted the coypu every few years when we knew we were approaching our limit.

Ella looked out into the bayou. "As long as we're careful, we might be able to go hunting for one tonight."

"What about the Bigfoot?" I asked hesitantly. We knew nothing about the creature.

"We saw it in the middle of the day, so maybe it will be asleep if we wait until well after dark," Ella said logically.

"You're not just saying that because you want to try killing it, are you?" Theia asked.

"No, I don't kill just for the fun of it, you know that," she said, a touch of bitterness in her voice.

"That doesn't mean that you aren't hoping it gives us a reason," Theia mumbled.

"Fine, then we don't need to go hunt the fucking coypu, happy?" Ella snapped.

"I think we do," I interjected, hating the itch in my throat.

"Ella, you're probably right about Bigfoot. If we wait until a few hours after dark, then we should be safe," Theia said, as close to an apology as she was likely to get.

"Thanks, hoe," Ella said, calming down.

"Welcome, bitch," Theia tossed back. I glanced at my sisters. The three of us were so different, but nothing could come between us.

Chapter 3

Kassie…

We cleaned up, washed away the blood from our processing station, and tossed the scraps in the freezer to be taken to the gator farm at the end of the month. Just because the gators didn't like us didn't mean we couldn't feed them our leftovers. The three of us ate dinner and sat down to watch some women's cage fighting to kill time before going out into the swamp. Ella and Theia yelled at the TV while I sat cross-legged on the couch, eating dates for the next few hours.

Well after dark, we dressed in our old jeans, mud boots, tank tops, and headlamps. Theia and I both grabbed guns and a machete each. Ella had multiple blades of varying sizes strapped to her legs and a machete in her hand as we walked out the door. Stopping on the edge of the tree line, we listened to our surroundings and exchanged looks.

When none of us heard anything other than swamp sounds, we went forward into the darkness of the trees, the smell of rotting vegetation filling our noses. Frogs croaked, and an owl's hoot sounded in the distance as crickets chirped. The nighttime swamp was unconcerned with our intrusion as we trudged deeper into the muck.

"Do we risk singing and drawing it in?" I asked in a hushed voice, not wanting to chase anything away.

"I'm more concerned with drawing in gators right now," Theia said in an equally low voice.

As Theia and I reasoned out why singing was a bad idea on a nighttime hunt, Ella began vocalizing a hauntingly beautiful tune with no name. Every time our sister used her power, there were no words. Theia and I were caught off guard momentarily and simply looked at her. A rustling in the distance drew our attention back to our surroundings. I raised my gun and nodded to Theia, who lifted her machete. Ella continued to vocalize, blades at the ready, as Theia eased toward the tall weeds.

What lashed out of the tall weeds wasn't a gator, coypu, or Bigfoot. Theia screamed and slashed at the monstrosity lunging for her. Ella charged forward, her vocalization forgotten. Fear and excitement at the sight of the monster licked up my spine. With my machete in hand, I charged at the Grunch that was attacking my sister.

The horrible-looking creature slashed out with its clawed hands, its leathery skin gleaming in the moonlight. It's twisted, goat-like face snarling and snapping at Theia's blade. Its red eyes glowed with an unnatural light as it twisted and kicked off the ground with its hooved back feet, jumping over us and twisting to attack from the back. The ape-like reptilian slashed out and caught my ankle, taking me off my feet. My mouth and nose filled with muddy swamp water, the smell of rotting vegetation nearly choking me as I struggled to regain my footing.

I pulled my face from the muck in time to see Ella slice off the horrible creature's arm as it was reaching for me. A terrifying screech tore from the creature's throat as it staggered backward. Ella planted her feet firmly in front of me, putting herself between me and the creature as Theia yanked me to my feet.

"Come and get some ugly," Ella said in a nearly gleeful voice.

"Ella," Theia said as she and I looked around and spotted two more sets of eyes, "it's not alone."

I pulled my shotgun up and aimed. "Fuck this shit," I said and shot the one that charged out of the darkness from the left.

"One arm is mine," Ella snarled and charged forward.

The one I'd shot staggered back, screeched its terrifying sound, and charged forward again. Their screams were blood-chilling, even to immortals. To humans, the fear the noise caused was utterly debilitating. Taking aim and fighting the chills from its screech, I shot again at the creature's head, blowing away half its skull. Tossing down the gun, I charged forward with my machete and hacked its hideous head from its body. Another set of glowing red eyes emerged out of the darkness as I slipped backward and twisted to face the new foe.

Ella's gleeful cackle and Theia's egging on of the Grunch she was facing filled the night air behind me. As I went to move forward and engage the fourth Grunch, the mud of the swamp sucked my boot from my foot, and I lurched sideways into the mud. My heart pounded in my ears, breathing heavily in my chest as I struggled to regain footing. My machete slashed through the air at the Grunch, and it jumped with its goat-like hind legs right over my blade.

Just before the disfigured monstrosity could lunge for me again, Bigfoot crashed through the swamp and slammed it into a tree so hard that it fell, and splinters exploded like confetti. My eyes widened in shock as a hand wrapped around my arm and yanked me to my feet. "Run!" Theia barked as she pulled me from the battle zone. Ella was next to us in seconds, glancing behind us as we ran clumsily through the swamp, our feet catching in the unseen mud of the night.

As we cleared the trees, coming into the light of the manor, we all stopped and turned to look back at the bayou we'd hunted in for years. My chest burned as I fought to catch my breath. My heart was pounding in my ears, and pain burned up my leg. I hissed in pain and looked down at my leg. Blood poured out of the back of my mud-covered calf and the side of my ankle, my boot completely missing, lost to the slime of the swamp.

"No wonder I couldn't stay on my fucking feet." I bitched.

Ella held up the horrifying head of the Grunch she'd attacked and smiled. "When you're all healed up, I'll let you kick the bastard back into the bayou."

"So are we not going to talk about how Bigfoot just exploded a fucking tree with that last Grunch?" Theia asked as she wrapped my arm around her neck and helped me into the house.

"That was pretty fucking awesome," Ella said, her voice tinted with excitement.

"Try fucking terrifying, thanks to the damn screeching of those Grunches," I mumbled. I hated being afraid.

Ella shrugged. "Fear is just an adrenaline rush for me."

"We know," Theia said as she glanced at the head Ella was still packing. "Do you really need to keep that thing?"

"She sure as hell does. That's the bastard that tore my Achilles tendon and shredded my calf. I'm going to mutilate that cock sucker," I seethed.

Theia chuckled. "It's so cute when you get hurt; you get all pissy and vengeful."

"Unlike normally, when she's all sweet and mild," Ella said as she tossed the head up and caught it like a bloody, rotten egg-smelling ball.

"Just because I'm not always in a bad mood or looking for a fight like the two of you, doesn't mean I don't have a dark side," I defended, watching my sister play with her prize.

"Ella, could you do me a favor and leave the head on the porch until you get a bag to put it in? I don't feel like cleaning up the blood tonight, and Kassie needs this taken care of before her skin grows back over whatever nastiness is caught inside the wound," Theia said as she looked at the head in disgust.

"Sure thing. I'll bag it and freeze it after we doctor-up Sandy," Ella said with a smile as she dropped the head next to the door.

"Fuck you, I killed one and was about to face down another with this mess of an ankle!" I defended.

"You really don't handle pain well," Theia muttered as she steered me towards the bathroom.

***

The next morning I was woken up by Ella sitting on my bed with a cup of coffee. Rubbing my eyes, I poked the button on the side of my phone to see that it was four in the morning. Glaring at my sister, I rolled over and pulled the blankets over my head. "I was injured last night, you know. Letting me sleep for another two hours would be very considerate of you," I muttered from under the covers.

"I'll have to move the bodies before then, or they'll draw gators," she said absently.

Poking my head out from under the covers, I frowned and looked up at her. "Bodies?"

She took a drink of her coffee, in no hurry to elaborate. "We have not four, but five dead bodies laying at the edge of the bayou."

I sat up, and she handed me my coffee before heading for the door. "You're just going to drop that on me and walk out?"

She paused at the door. "You should be healed enough to walk with a limp out to the porch," she said, turning and walking away.

Groaning, I threw back the blankets and got out of bed gingerly. The pain in my ankle was bearable. Part of me wished she'd at least taken my coffee out for me, but Ella wasn't the nurturing type. As I got to my feet, hot coffee splashing from the side of my mug onto the floor, Theia walked in and took my cup. "Thanks," I said, knowing she wouldn't help me outside, not that I wanted her to.

"I don't know why she didn't just put it in a travel mug; you wouldn't have made a mess that way," Theia said as she stuck close but offered no assistance. My sisters had learned long ago that making me feel weaker by providing help when I didn't ask for it only got them hit. Not that they were any different.

Looking down at the wet spot on the floor, I grabbed the bloody towel that had been under my ankle as I slept and tossed it on the light brown liquid. "There, problem solved."

Theia rolled her eyes. "Just come look so Ella and I can get the mess cleaned up before sunrise. I don't want some random human showing up and seeing it."

"You want me to hack up your ankle and calf!" I snapped.

"Sorry, Kassie, you'll understand when you see," Theia said, backing down.

Narrowing my eyes, I looked at her as I limped by and out of the bedroom. It wasn't like my sister to back down from an easy argument. Gritting my teeth, I braced myself on the wall just halfway through the living room. *Breathe.* I let go of the wall and limped the rest of the way, out the door and onto the porch, where I squinted into the darkness at the lumps scattered near the edge of the tree line.

"And I present to you, Bigfoot's warning of coming into his new favorite territory," Ella said as she turned a spotlight onto the massacre lining the trees. My mouth fell open as I looked at the dismembered bodies littering the ground. "From the looks of it, there are five dead Grunch. That one there is the one I killed, that one is yours, and that one is Theia's handy work," Ella said as she moved from one mangled body to another. "This one is covered in splinters and moss, so I think it's the last one we saw before leaving last night. That one there must have shown up after we left."

"I think I'm going to be sick," I muttered as I sank down, my back against the wall, glad I didn't have to get any closer to the smell.

Theia handed me my cup of coffee. "The smell is pretty bad. They seem to stink worse when they are dead, even from this distance."

"For once, I'm almost glad to be injured," I said, feeling a little guilty that my sisters had to clean up the mess without me.

"I vote we just pile them up and burn them," Ella said as she turned back to look at us.

Theia made a face. "Do you think it will make the smell worse?"

Ella tossed her hands up. "How am I supposed to know? I've never burnt a Grunch before; I just don't want to have to find a place to bury the fuckers before sunrise."

"I'm not roasting marshmallows over them, so don't ask," Theia said as she walked off the porch, predicting Ella's dark humor.

"You're no fun," Ella shot back.

Looking down at my bandaged wound, I reached down and peeled back the taped gauze pad. My skin was angry and puckered, like a wound that had just had stitches a few days ago. "Is it sad that I'm a little bitter Bigfoot stole my revenge," I called out as I pulled the rest of the blood-soaked bandage from my leg. By tomorrow morning, it would look like nothing more than a scratch if any marks were left.

"I still got the head in the freezer for you," Ella called out as she dragged one of the bodies over to the pile she and Theia were forming.

"You can have the honor of lighting this shit if you can hobble your ass down here," Theia added as she coughed, the smell getting to her.

"Hard pass," I called back, sipping my coffee. My thoughts were firing one after another. Was this Bigfoot's way of telling us to stay out of his swamp? Was the creature telling us to clean up after ourselves? Or was this his way of making a truce with us? In all the years we'd hunted this area, we'd never found any trace of a Grunch. "Hey, what if Bigfoot was actually after that pack of Grunch and this is his way of saying thanks?" I called out as I watched them work.

Theia stopped and frowned up at me. "What makes you think this is a thank you?"

"If it is, I approve," Ella said, obviously enjoying the carnage.

"Think about it: how long have we been hunting this swamp? We've never found any evidence of Bigfoot or a Grunch until a few days ago. Plus, from what he did to that tree, I'd say the three of us didn't look like much of an obstacle to him that first day that he just left us in the swamp." I explained.

"So, do you think our Bigfoot problems are over?" Theia called back as she picked up a leg, grabbed the arm of another body, and began to drag it to the pile.

"How am I supposed to know? It's just a theory," I called back.

"I'd say we should just keep hunting elsewhere for a few weeks, maybe even a month," Ella said as she walked over to another body. We fell silent as they finished cleaning up and set them ablaze. As we drank our coffee, the three of us sat on the porch and watched the putrid fire, grateful that the heat didn't increase the smell. After I'd finished the cup of coffee Ella had brought me, I'd made my way back to bed, the healing process leaving me exhausted.

Glowing red eyes loomed in the darkness, and I held my machete ready for the Grunch I knew lurked in the brush. However, what came out of the thick weeds and bushes wasn't a Grunch but a fully nude male. My mouth went dry at the sight of him, his face unimportant as his muscled body moved forward, his throbbing cock

ready to give me the release I so craved. Another male came out of the

darkness behind me and ran his hand up the front of my throat, locking

his hand around the bottom of my jaw as the other hand slipped

between my legs, my clothes had vanished from my body.

"Let us please you." The male in front of me said as he reached

us. His hands began to roam my body as the one behind me kissed and

nipped at my throat. I let them take me to the swampy earth, one behind

and one in front, their eyes glowing red in the dark mist that rose

around us. Claw-tipped hands gripped my hips as one male took me

from behind, and the other drove himself between my lips.

In one solid motion, that vivid image was distorted as they were

pulled from my body and morphed into the horrid creatures I had

initially feared. They lunged for me, their claws slashing at my naked

body, my guts spilling from me as I screamed.

The next thing I knew, I jerked awake in bed, panting from the

dream. Had I really just dreamed about fucking the Grunch? Putting my

head in my hands, I recalled my dream. No, and yes, I had dreamed

about fucking them, but they weren't Grunch when we'd fucked. Tears

streamed down my face in self-disgust and frustration. I don't know how long I sat there, enveloped in the darkness, silently crying, before I

could finally find solace in sleep.

Chapter 4

Kassie…

As 7:00 a.m. approached, I pulled on my old mud boots over my still-sore ankle to walk out the door with my sisters. By the end of the day my ankle would feel like nothing had happened. My anger at the Grunch that had sliced open my calf and ankle had been rekindled when I'd had to slip my feet into the uncomfortable pair of old boots that leaked. Thanks to the disfigured monster, my feet would be waterlogged and blistered before the soreness of my ankle entirely dissipated. My anger at the creature was so great that I'd turned back from the door, grabbed the head out of the freezer, and stabbed at it repeatedly in the sink with an icepick before shoving it back into the freezer.

Clay was already at the dock waiting on us when we arrived, as he had been two days prior. His smile of welcome faltered slightly as we grew closer. "What's got you in such a bad mood," he wrinkled his nose, "and what is that smell?"

Theia glanced at me before answering him, "She had a bunch of eggs bust on her this morning and lost her good boots."

"Those were my favorite mud boots," I grumbled.

"Would it improve your mood if I told you I brought a book you might like? I've already finished it and thought I might see if you'd like to give it a try." Reaching under his seat, he pulled out a book and offered it to me.

I offered him a weak smile. "Thanks, but I'm going to be in a bad mood until my new boots come in," I said, taking the book and looking at the title. "I actually haven't read this one yet, either. I'll see if I can pick it up at the library later this week."

"You don't have to do that; just borrow my copy," he said as he turned and started up the boat.

As much as I still wanted to be angry, Clay's gesture had lightened my mood slightly. As we maneuvered the waterways of the bayou, my sisters' and I sat quietly on the boat. We stopped in the same place we had two days ago. With the fan silenced, the sound of cicadas filled the humid air, and in the distance, I could hear the calls of a whippoorwill. "Thank you. We'll be back in a few hours or sooner if all goes well," I said to Clay as I stepped off the boat to help my sister's hunt.

"Now that you're done talking to the help, why don't you make yourself useful and sing in some dinner," Ella said bitterly as I caught up with them.

"Fuck you too, Ella," I shot back, the start of my good mood gone.

"The sooner we can find a coypu, the sooner we can get home and be done with the damned mortal," she said in a harsh tone as we made our way deeper into the bayou. "Tomorrow, we can just go back to hunting our own slice of the swamp land. It's like you said, we never saw those Grunch before Bigfoot came around; now that they are taken care of, the beast can be on his way."

"And what if I was wrong?" I asked through gritted teeth, the stinging in my ankle annoying me.

"Then I'll kill the swamp ape," she said simply.

"He turned a tree into confetti with a Grunch; I don't think taking on said swamp ape is advisable," Theia chimed in, glancing at me.

"You and I both know she's not going to listen to reason. If she thinks she can take a creature we know nothing about, then she's going to do it. I just hope we can save her stubborn ass," I said in response to Theia's look.

"The next sound coming out of your mouth should be a fucking melody," Ella snapped at me.

"Doe-rae-me," I said in a bland tone.

"Fa-so-la-tea-da," Theia added in the same bland tone, both of us fed up with Ella's bitching.

Ella turned to glare at us when her eyes got huge. "Duck!" She yelled and threw her machete without hesitation. Theia and I dropped, then spun to see the blade hit a cottonmouth, sticking the nearly seven-foot-long creature to a tree, the thump of the impact echoing in the surrounding trees. Its massive body thrashed and twisted around as blood spilled from the wound, lasting only moments before going limp in death's grip. "Too fucking easy," she grumbled as she marched by us and yanked her blade from the tree, wiping the blood on her pants.

"Does that mean we're done?" Theia demanded as Ella hacked off the snake's head.

"I came out here looking for a fucking coypu; what the hell do you think?" Ella snapped.

"What the hell? You're not the one with leaky old boots and a still healing ankle; why don't you stop snapping at us for a few minutes so that we can be quiet enough to actually catch something?" I shot back before Theia could say anything. The tension that flowed from my sisters' was as heavy as the humidity in the Louisiana swamp.

"Just stop asking stupid questions," Ella finally snapped as she stored the headless body in her bag and impaled the head on a branch so no one would step on the venom-filled fangs.

We trudged through the swamp in silence until we were far enough away that Clay wouldn't hear any of us sing. Seeing as my ankle was still healing, I was again given vocal duty, clearly in no shape to be helping further. Only scratching the surface of my siren's call, I sang a soothing tune, drawing in something gray in the distance. It wasn't long before we were stuffing two opossums into our bag. We continued to hunt for a coypu for another hour before turning back in the direction of the boat. It would be nearing three in the afternoon by the time we got back to the manor, and our kills needed to be cleaned before they grew rancid.

"I know you'll turn me down, but my momma raised me to offer help," Clay said as he stood and walked to the edge of the boat, seeing us coming out of the trees.

"Thanks anyway," I said with a weak smile.

"Once you get on the boat, why don't you take those waterlogged boots off and empty them out? Your feet may just dry out by the time we get back to your manor," Clay said, nodding to my squishing feet.

"That sounds amazing," I said as I got on the boat and plopped down. I pulled off one boot, and before I could get the other off, Clay was already dumping the water over the edge and handing it back to me. "Um, thanks."

"I didn't want the water all over inside the boat," he said with a wink.

"What he means to say is get yourself some new boots and stop filling his precious boat with swamp water," Theia said as she flopped down in the boat. Ella rolled her eyes and sat next to her.

"Something like that," Clay said with a good-natured smile. "Looks like y'all had some luck today," he added, nodding at the bags Ella and Theia had between their feet.

"No questions, remember," I reminded him with narrowed eyes.

"I was only remarking on your obvious success in today's endeavor, leading to my next question of when do you think you'll require my services next?" he elaborated as he maneuvered around me to start the boat.

Pursing my lips, I glanced at my sisters to see Ella glaring daggers at Clay while Theia cleaned chunks of mud and leaves from her tangled ponytail. "I suppose a couple of days from now," I said over the fan's noise.

"Three days and I'll be open to new clients, fella's gotta make a living," Clay said in response.

"Sounds fair to me," I told him.

"You should tell your sister that wearing a hat might help keep stuff out of her hair; it's what my sister does," Clay told me, working around one of the rules I'd given him upon contracting his services.

"You should tell the boatman that I don't like hats or tricksters," Theia said, her eyes narrowing.

Sighing heavily, I looked at Clay and said, "I've offered to braid it for her to help, but she's stubborn and wild. I think she may even like pulling things out of her hair."

"So what did you think of that book we both were somehow reading?" Clay asked, changing the subject.

"It was good but a bit predictable. What about the one you said you'd loan me?" I asked.

"It's less predictable, but if you don't contact me in three days, then you can drop it off at the docks when you finish it or just keep it. I've read it a few times already," he told me, his smile kind in his handsome face. Looking at him, I took in his features for the first time. He had a playful cockiness about him, his chin strong, his lips fuller than most, a light brown beard enhancing his jawline, upper lip, and chin. *Gods, I bet that would feel good between my thighs.* His cheekbones were high, and his brows dark. His hair was a rich brown, left slightly longer and a bit messy, lending a wildness to his appearance. His shoulders were broad, supporting his six-foot frame. His legs were thick under his jeans, leading me to believe he spent a good deal of time exercising them. Catching myself, I looked out at the water and away from the male before me.

"I'm actually thinking about reading a different genre next," I said, no longer wanting to borrow his book.

"I brought this one for you. If you don't want it, then I can donate it to the library," Clay said with a frown.

"I guess if you're going to get rid of it anyway, I'll give it a try. I'll just make the next book a new genre," I said, feeling awkward. We fell into silence for the remainder of the trip, the sound of the boat drowning out the noise of the bayou.

Chapter 5

Kassie...

"I hope to hear from you in the next few days. Maybe you can recommend another book. Most of my other employers don't read much," Clay said with a smile before starting his boat back up and heading off. I turned and walked toward the manor with Theia; Ella was already yards away.

"If you feel the itch, why not just scratch it with the boatman," Theia asked, nodding toward the fan boat that was disappearing down the waterway.

"It's not a good idea to mix business with pleasure," I told her with a glare. The truth was that I was afraid I was getting too close to him. In my twelve-thousand years, every time I'd gotten close to a male, they had been taken from me. Clay was an innocent human who didn't deserve what fate dealt those closest to me.

Theia shrugged. "He's handsome enough; maybe he can help me take the edge off."

My hands clenched into fists, and I could feel my lips twitching into a snarl before I quickly reigned myself in.

Theia smiled knowingly. "You don't have to always hide from me. Ella and I both know you're the sensitive one. No matter how many lovers are taken from you, we will always be here for you."

Letting out a sigh, I closed my eyes and nodded before looking up at her with a smile. "The three of us for eternity."

"You can always try Ella's method of coping," Theia said, looking at our sister.

Following her gaze, I looked where Ella stood, cleaning the opossums. "We both know that her method is dangerous."

"Yes, but at least it's rare that she loses control," Theia said with a shrug.

I sighed. I could always find a female to satisfy my urges, but it always left me feeling wrong. While I found them attractive, it wasn't so much a sexual attraction as it was an admiration of their charms. Throughout my life, males had been the only ones to leave me mostly satisfied instead of somewhat, but even those encounters had been rare. Theia and Ella had been with more females than males; since coming into our powers, Ella had been with only females. "We should go help her instead of standing here talking."

"She's been in such a bad mood since contracting Clay that I don't want to help her," Theia said bitterly but began walking toward Ella anyway.

"If the two of you are done discussing the meat, maybe you could help me process our dinner," Ella snapped as we approached her. The fight with the Grunch only days ago had apparently worn off, and she was itching for more confrontation.

"Does it piss you off that he's actually a likable male or that he's yet to give you a reason to kill him?" I asked, doing little to keep the bitterness out of my tone.

"I think she just needs to get laid, and he's not a female," Theia said as she picked up the second opossum.

Before either of us could see it coming, Ella had punched Theia in the face, knocking her on her ass. Rolling my eyes, I snagged the opossums and got out of the way. Theia was on her feet before I'd even gotten the first opossum picked up, and the fight was on. Luckily, the three of us were excellent fighters, and as long as I didn't get in the way, they wouldn't hit me by mistake. I'd learned long ago not to break them up unless it got out of hand. This was Ella's biggest drawback; outbursts of physical violence.

Staying close, I took over cleaning our kills while keeping an eye on my sisters. It would only be a matter of time before I found myself in a fight with one or both of them in the near future. We were all feeling the itch in our throats, and the longer we denied it, the more on edge we would get, much like a human would get hangry. By the time I'd finished processing our kills, Theia and Ella were bloody, bruised, and not speaking as they helped clean each other up. Helping to doctor one another after a fight was how we apologized and thanked each other for the fight, which helped blow off some steam.

After dinner that night, Ella went up to her room, where I knew I would hear the shower in about five or six hours. Theia turned on the Xbox and popped in her headset, connecting with her black ops friends across the country while I ran the dishwasher. Leaning forward on the sink after pressing start, I closed my eyes. The itch in my throat had been getting worse for the last week. I'd sung in our kill twice now, so I wasn't sure why it was so bad. I opened my eyes and glanced toward the living room, where Theia yelled at the TV. With a sigh, I dried my hands and decided to go for one of my walks as I picked up the shotgun.

I walked out of the kitchen door and down to the water's edge, the manor with its great white pillars glowing behind me. I walked down the dock and sat, watching the fireflies and listening to the frogs. The music of the bayou helped to calm me. Closing my eyes, I listened closely to the sounds around me to be sure the sounds of water on a boat weren't one of them. Once I was confident that it was only bayou sounds, I began to sing 'Down in New Orleans.'

It wasn't long before a figure appeared across the water, causing me to grab my gun. I watched closely and my singing stopped as Bigfoot stood on the far bank. Then he sank to the ground and leaned back against a tree, never taking his eyes off me. We stared at each other for what felt like an eternity before I finally sat back down on the dock, laying the gun down next to me. He seemed utterly unphased by the weapon.

Biting my lip, I looked around, then back at Bigfoot. "Hey, big fella, let's make a deal; I won't shoot you as long as you stay on your side of the water, deal?" I asked, not expecting an answer, but then he did something completely unexpected. He raised a hand to his mouth, tapping his lips, then gestured at me. My eyes widened. "Did you just ask me to sing?" He nodded. I swallowed, ignoring the burning in my throat. "Alright, but just one song, then I need to go," I started over singing my song and watched as he leaned his head back against the tree and closed his eyes.

When I finished my song, he opened his eyes and sat forward. "You probably don't understand me, but I really shouldn't sing any more tonight, but I can talk for a little while if you just want some company?" I wasn't sure why I was talking to him, as I wasn't even sure he understood anything I was saying. He just stared at me, so I sighed and decided to speak to him. "My sisters got into a fight today. No one lost any teeth this time, so I guess it wasn't that bad of a fight really. I just have a feeling that I'll be the next to snap if I don't find a way to blow off some steam soon."

He leaned forward, resting his arms on bent knees and looking at me. Could he actually understand me? I had to wonder how many people had talked to a Bigfoot. As far as I knew, they were just as elusive in the immortal community as they were in the human. "I'm what you call a Siren. I don't know if you know what that is; most don't understand what that means. They just think we sing to entrap males and make them do our bidding, but in reality, we don't always have a choice. We get this itch or burn in our throat, demanding that we satisfy our urges, or the Siren Call comes out to force someone else. Building a relationship with anyone is dangerous because we're hated and immortal," I smiled as I said that last part.

Glancing back at the mansion, I thought about the only lasting relationship any of us would ever have. "At least I have my sisters, no matter what. We fight and argue, but are always there for one another." I looked back at Bigfoot. "We were separated once, for many years, but that was before we had our powers. Once we found each other again, we vowed never to let anyone separate us again; never let anyone hurt us again." I looked down at my knees, thinking about all the pain I'd felt in my long life and how they had always been there for me. "Well, that's enough chatter for tonight," I said with a smile. "Thank you for staying on your side of the water. Oh, and thank you for helping us take on the five Grunch. My ankle got scratched, or I would have been more help. It's all healed now; the perks of being immortal." He rose to his feet, and I tensed, adrenaline flooding my body, ready for a fight, but he just turned and walked away into the trees.

Getting to my feet, I turned and headed back to the manor. When I walked in, Theia was still yelling into her headset, and Ella's room was as silent as the grave. Walking into the living room, I picked up Clay's book he had given me and curled up in my favorite chair. The book was my key to travel, exploration, and adventure. I wanted to be as brave as the characters in those pages, but because we were what we were, me and my sisters had to stay quiet and blend in with the rest of humanity as boring and uninteresting. When Theia plugged in her headset, she was out of this little town. Ella was the only one who didn't seem bothered by us not being able to travel openly and experience everything the world has to offer.

After a few more hours, the sound of the shower water running told me Ella was ready to join us once again, her nightly coping done with. It was thirty minutes before she came down the steps, picked up her tactical gear magazine, and sat next to Theia. She would read an article or two while Theia finished whatever mission she was on, and then we would find something to watch on TV. Closing my book, I looked around our living room, taking in the dingy paint and the worn-down furniture. "It won't be long before we need to move on from this place." We'd been here, existing like this for nearly fifteen years.

"We should be able to stay a few more years; we just need to travel one town further for things so they don't notice our lack of wrinkles," Ella said in an uninterested tone, her voice distorted from her still-healing vocal cords. It was just like her to have no urge to move, to find something new. I sighed and turned my attention to Theia's game. Once it was over, Ella turned on 'The L Word,' and I watched one episode with them before I got up and went to bed, two in the morning being my limit.

I sank deeper into the softness of my bed, the sheets clinging to my overheated body. The itch in my throat intensified, a constant reminder of the restless desire that consumed me. Unable to ignore the throbbing ache any longer, I decided to surrender to my own touch. As I closed my eyes, a rush of anticipation coursed through me, my mind focused solely on the sensations that awaited. My hand ventured between my legs, feeling the familiar warmth and wetness that signaled my arousal. With each stroke, I could feel the slickness of my own desire coating my fingers, making them glide effortlessly over my sensitive flesh. I circled my clit with deliberate precision, the pleasure building with each touch. Seeking more, my other hand found solace on my breast, squeezing it firmly, the pressure sending jolts of electricity throughout my body. The tension continued to mount, a relentless wave threatening to consume me entirely. My fingers delved deeper, plunging in and out, their movements becoming more urgent, more desperate. I experimented with different rhythms, flicking and pinching, exploring every inch of my desire, determined to find the release I craved. And then, as if the universe aligned in my favor, I felt it - the electrifying surge of pleasure that washed over me, bringing me to the pinnacle of ecstasy. In that moment, my mind conjured vivid images of the boatman, his rugged beard grazing against my tender skin, heightening the intensity of my climax. With the release of my pent-up desire, a sense of tranquility washed over me, lulling me into a deep and restful sleep.

Chapter 6

Twelve thousand years ago…

"I love you, Kassandra. You and only you," Naoki said before he kissed me as we stood in the quiet sandstone corridor.

I hadn't thought to find happiness after being separated from my sisters all those years ago. It was true the Queen had smiled upon me, but to find love! "I love you as well, Naoki," I said as he broke the kiss.

"How sweet," the Queen's voice made us jump, and I spun to face her. "Naoki, you always have told the prettiest lies," she said as she stood there, her lavender dress pristine and stitched in gold, her hair braided and perfectly pinned. She was ten years or more older than me, but she was stunning nonetheless.

He stepped forward, lacing his fingers with mine. "Forgive me my Queen, but I am not lying to Kassandra."

Her full lips tilted downward into a frown before her expression became thoughtful. "Kassandra, my sweet child, do you believe him?"

I looked at Naoki; he was just taller than me, his skin golden and beautiful from the sun, and his hair hung in dark curls to his ears. "I do, My Queen," I answered honestly, knowing the penalty for lying. "When your soldiers first found me, I was filled with fear. Fear of the things I did not yet know, of how we would be treated. When you chose me, I realized that I had been wrong to fear for myself. You have been kind to me, and in your service, I have found true happiness with Naoki," Naoki smiled, his amber eyes glinting with happiness.

"Did you know that Naoki has been my lover for nearly eleven moons now? Did you know that the only reason you crossed paths is because he's been slipping into my bedchamber at night and making love to me? Oh," she paused briefly, before continuing, "there were times in the gardens and the throne room when the king was out in the city taking care of some petty quarrel or other business. Do you still believe he loves you and only you?" Her mouth turned upwards into a mocking smirk.

I hesitated before I glanced at the male, who had become my lover for the last week. "It's the reason I'd told him no before, the reason we had both denied ourselves for so long," I admitted, being open and honest with my Queen, who had been so kind to me, even in her strictness at times. After all, she'd been sure none of the whippings had left scars.

"My Queen, we cannot remain lovers; we knew that from the start, that should the king ever find out, we would both perish. Kassandra and I, are of similar stations, so when I discovered I loved *her, I thought it wisest to tell her of my feelings before another could take her affections; I was going to tell you tonight that I can no longer be with you when my heart belongs to another," Naoki told her with a quick smile at me.*

The Queen smiled, and in a sweet tone addressed Naoki, "Naoki, if that's how you truly feel then who am I to stand in your way?" She then turned to me and instructed, "Kassandra, I want you to go and put on your finest clothing and have one of the other servants help you with your hair, tell them I said to be sure it will rival only mine, then meet me in the courtyard as the sun hits the highest point. Naoki, come with me so that I can prepare you for later, we will celebrate the love of my most cherished servant."

"Thank you! Thank you, my Queen!" I exclaimed as I quickly kissed Naoki and hurried off to prepare for the celebration. I'd feared she wouldn't understand, or forbid it, but her reaction filled me with joy.

Later that day, as I was making my way to the courtyard, the flowering vines wrapped around the pillars of the shaded pathway leading along the edge of the palace.

As I was nearing the courtyard when a guard approached me. "Kassandra," he asked, uncertain. Most of the guards had not bothered to learn any of the servants' names, even the ones they'd slept with.

"Yes," I said with a smile, wondering if the Queen had sent him to escort me.

"You are under arrest for conspiring against our King and Queen," he said as he grabbed me by my wrist roughly.

"What? No! I haven't done anything! Please, there must be some mistake!" I pleaded as I pried at his bruising grip.

"Save it for the Queen," he said as he dragged me into the courtyard.

"The Queen? But I've done nothing wrong! I just spoke with her only hours ago," I pleaded looking over to see her standing near the iron bull. "No, please, what have I done?" I pleaded with the guard and pulled on his hold, nearly toppling him.

"Be still!" He snapped. He then shoved me forward, and I fell to my knees where another guard quickly shackled my wrists, the noon sun casting no shadow on the hot stone pavers.

I looked up at the Queen. "What is going on?" I asked, tears streaming down my face.

"Your lover, Naoki, has been found guilty of conspiring against my husband and me. He claims he was doing it for you. Is this true?" the Queen demanded, her elegant face impassive as she stood at the bottom of the steps.

"What? No! Why would I betray you?" I asked, glancing behind her at the guards dragging a fighting Naoki forward. "Naoki!" I yelled and shot to my feet, only to be yanked back down by my chains.

"Do you confirm that he is your lover?" demanded the Queen.

"Yes, you know this; we only want to be together," I said as I watched the guards force him into the bull.

"Kassandra! Kassandra, forgive me!" He yelled from inside the bull, pounding on its great iron insides.

"What did he do? Why are we being punished?" I sobbed and looked up at the Queen, a slight smile on her face.

"Your lover was planning on killing my husband to free your sister, a woman he's never set eyes on. Therefore, he had to be planning this horrible thing for you," she looked at the guards before ordering, "Light it." She looked back at me, her ghost of a smile gone. "Do you believe he loves you now?" With that, she turned away from me, her robes fluttering in the air as she made her way to the steps.

"No! Naoki!" I cried as they lit the fire. I screamed and cried as he burned, the smell of his burnt flesh filling the air, until finally, his screams became silent. I looked up at the smiling Queen, watching me from the top of the steps, as tears streamed down my face. I gave into the strange itch in my throat then, letting out a scream that ripped through the courtyard in waves. "Let me go." The guard that had been standing next to me turned to me and released my shackles, my siren's call resonating from deep inside my throat for the first time. My breathing ragged from my cries. "Kill the Queen," I said without flinching; my cheeks chapped from the tears, and my voice hoarse from screaming.

I sat straight up in my bed, my heart pounding in my ears, tears streaming down my face. I was back in the present; my dream was a vivid memory of what had happened all those years ago. The pain of my first lover lost stung now as it had that very day. The itch in my throat roared as my sorrow surged. I threw back the blankets, wiping the salty tears from my face, and staggered out of my room, through the dark living room, and into the kitchen. Choking back my tears with a loud sniff, I threw open the freezer door. The bitter air flowed gently out, and the sound of the ice cracking at the rapid change of temperature greeted me. I reached in and pulled out the bottle of whiskey, took the lid off immediately, and took a long drink as I let the door fall shut on the freezer.

Closing my eyes, I embraced the new burning sensation, the burn I'd chosen. Opening my eyes, I looked back at the freezer, realizing there was one more coping method I could add to this night. Tipping the bottle back again, I reopened the freezer and pulled out the Grunch head. "Hello, ugly," I muttered through the burn and stench. The freezer door closed and fell shut with a soft smack. I turned to walk out the door with my rotten-smelling friend, only to find Ella standing on the other side, taking a drink of her beer. "Got a gun out there with you?"

She lowered the beer and nodded, opening the door for me without a word. I walked by her and out into the yard. Plopping the head down on the moss-covered lawn, I made my way back to the side patio, where my sister held out a gun with one hand and tipped back a long neck with the other. Once I took the gun from her, she leaned against the side of the house and crossed her arms. "Memories suck ass," she said flatly.

"Naoki," I responded, holding the whiskey out to her. Once she'd taken it, I turned back to the rancid-smelling head and aimed the gun. "Fuck Atlantis," I said as I squeezed the trigger and watched as the head exploded and rolled back on the mossy lawn.

"Fuck Atlantis," Ella said as I turned around and took the bottle back.

Lights flipped on inside as the thumping of Theia's running filled the now-silent night. Moments later, she threw open the door, her machete in hand. I toasted her with my bottle before tipping it back once again. "Fuck," she said, letting the door fall shut behind her as she turned back into the kitchen. I walked over and sank to the concrete patio, my back resting against the house. Theia came out with a bottle of vodka and sat down next to me, still in nothing but a tank top and panties. "Which one was it this time?"

I pursed my lips and swirled my bottle, watching the amber liquid glint in the faint light now coming from the kitchen. "Naoki."

"Shit," she said, then tipped back her bottle and took a long drink of her clear poison of choice.

We'd sat in the dim light for about ten minutes before Ella leaned forward and looked at Theia. "Is there going to be enough left for Bloody Marys in the morning, or are we having Irish coffee?"

"This is the last bottle of whiskey," I said, glancing up at her.

"There is a bottle of each under my bed," Theia said without looking at either of us.

"I've got a bottle of whiskey in my dresser," Ella added before taking another drink of her beer.

"I have a case of beer in my closet and a bottle of vodka," I admitted.

"Good to know we all support each other's bad habits," Theia said in a scoffing tone.

"Yep," I said as I took a swig from my bottle again and watched the lightning bugs blink until they became blurs.

"How long do you think it's going to be before Ares starts his shit again?" Theia asked, breaking the silence after just a few moments.

"He instigated both World Wars the last time. I honestly thought he was behind the Twin Towers," I said bluntly.

"I wonder if the mortals are making it hard for him in modern times?" She wandered absent-mindedly.

"I wish we could just track him down and end him already. It would give us one last thing to worry about." I hated that we were his playthings. He loved it when we lost control or when our anger led to bloodshed on a battlefield. Not that I didn't enjoy a good victory, just that I didn't like being manipulated.

"We will end him," Ella said bluntly into the dark. We fell into silence then, drinking in the darkness of the night.

***

"Rise and shine bitches," Ella said as she flipped the living room light on in our faces. Theia and I both groaned and covered our faces. Luckily for us, being immortal meant hangovers weren't a thing, but a lack of sleep due to a night of drinking until you passed out still made us cranky. I eyed the clock and groaned, noting it was only nine in the morning.

"How can you drink all night and still get up so damn early?" Theia complained.

"Sleep is weakness," Ella said as she sat down two bloody marys on the coffee table, topped with a boiled egg, bacon, and celery. "Breakfast," she said before walking back into the kitchen.

"Why is it that the only time she cooks for us is when one of us has a nightmare?" I muttered to Theia.

"Because it involves alcohol," Theia said as she sat up and grabbed her drink.

Sitting up, I grabbed my drink and plucked the bacon from the top. "I should go clean up the head after I eat," I said absently.

"You may just puke up that egg," Theia said, glancing at me from the corner of her eye.

"How is it that I have a stronger stomach than you," I asked with a smile.

"Maybe you just can't smell as well as I do," she tossed back.

"I already cleaned it up," Ella said as she returned with her drink.

"That was sweet of you," Theia said in a snarky tone.

"It was smart of me. The two of you are irresponsible drunks," she said flatly.

"Thank you," I said quietly, feeling guilty about leaving her to clean up my mess.

"I didn't say I cleaned up the bottles. That's up to you two. This makes us even for you cleaning the opossums," she told me as she curled her legs up under her in the chair.

"If I clean up the bottles, that makes us square, too," Theia said, pointing at me.

I frowned at her. "And dishes, all day."

"That's not fair," Theia complained.

"I had to clean three critters while the two of you let off steam. Plus, breakfast is next to no dishes," I countered.

"Fine," Theia huffed, rolling her eyes before shoving the whole boiled egg in her mouth. I looked at her in disgust before returning to my bloody mary. The memory of Naoki still tingled in the back of my mind as I swallowed down the spicy red beverage. Living in the present was much better than living in the past, but the past had a way of rearing its ugly head for all three of us.

Chapter 7

Kassie…

After dinner, Ella disappeared into her room, coping in private. Clay would arrive in the morning to take my sisters and me into the swamp to hunt, so drinking myself to sleep wasn't an option. "I'm going to the dock," I told Theia as she sat in front of her game after finishing the dishes.

"Take the shotgun to slow down Sasquatch; I'll be listening for the shot," she told me, knowing I wanted to be alone.

"Thanks, but I don't think he's going to hurt me as long as I don't piss him off and go into his territory."

"Just take the damn gun," she said with a glare.

Rolling my eyes, I picked it up from where it hung on the wall next to the kitchen and walked out the door. The sounds of crickets and frogs filled the night air as I made my way to the dock. Closing my eyes, I listened intently to my surroundings as always – just the sounds of nature. As I settled myself on the end of the dock, I leaned back against the post, rested the shotgun in my lap, and began to sing.

It wasn't long before Bigfoot came out of the trees and sat on the far side of the bank as he had before. Once I finished my song, I looked at him. He was staring back at me, with his amber eyes glinting in the moonlight. "Hey there, big fella; I hope my sisters and I didn't upset you last night," I said, not sure if he could understand a word I said.

He pointed at the gun in my lap and looked at me expectantly. "Are you asking if I'm going to shoot you?" To my surprise, he shook his head no. "Asking what I was shooting at last night?" I tried again. He nodded and leaned back against a tree facing me, his hands in his furry lap. "A Grunch's severed head. Ella cut the head off the one who sliced my tendon, and we wrapped it up and put it in the freezer so I could take my aggression out on it once I healed."

He tilted his head as if to question me further. "You know," I paused briefly, "trying to interpret what you want to say is kinda weird, right?" He just continued to look at me. With a sigh, I leaned my head back against the dock post. "Last night was a rough night. I took out my anger against the Grunch already by stabbing the head multiple times, but then last night, I had dreamt about someone I lost a long time ago, someone who was taken from me. When I shot the head, I wasn't seeing the Grunch; I was seeing her mocking face as she commanded those fires to be lit." A tear slipped down my cheek, and the sound of movement made me look up. Bigfoot was standing just at the water's edge, looking intently at me.

I jumped up to my feet and picked up the shotgun. "Remember our deal, big guy, you stay over there, and I won't shoot you." He reached up and touched his face as he pointed to me. "Tears of anger, not weakness," I grated out. "I won't ever be that weak again. No one will hurt me like that again."

He let out a low growl, then stepped back and looked into the trees. "What is it?" I asked, as if he could tell me. Suddenly, a coyote came charging out of the trees and barrelled right at Bigfoot. Without a moment of hesitation, I cocked the shotgun and was about to shoot when Bigfoot roared at the small animal. Immediately the coyote began yelping as it twisted and turned, fleeing back into the woods. The sound of birds taking off in the trees was followed by Bigfoot charging after the coyote.

Lowering the shotgun, I disarmed it and turned to walk back to the manor, only to see Theia charging out of the house. "Kassie! What was that?" She yelled as she ran over to me.

After I waved her off, she slowed down as I made my way over to her. "Bigfoot was sitting across from me at the dock when a coyote got his attention."

"Bigfoot!" She exclaimed in shock.

"Yeah, he was out here a few nights ago too. I think he's been keeping an eye on us for some reason."

"So you just come out here alone and sit with that thing?" She snapped angrily.

I shrugged. "Why not? He stays on his side of the water, and I stay on mine. I'm still trying to figure out whether he understands me or not."

She pinched the bridge of her nose. "I thought Ella and I were the crazy ones, but here you are talking to a seven-foot monster with unknown powers and aggression."

"How else are we supposed to learn anything about him?" I countered as we walked back to the house.

"Do we really need to learn anything about him?" She snapped, tossing her hands up in the air.

I shrugged. "I don't know. I guess I'm just bored. I'm going to take a shower and go to bed. We have to be up early anyway," I told her as I walked past her, clearly still fuming about the situation and into the house.

***

Five in the morning came early indeed. I woke to Ella sitting on my bed with a cup of coffee in hand and another cup on my nightstand. "Theia told me you've been talking to Bigfoot," she said without looking at me.

"I have the shotgun with me in case he tries to cross the water," I defended.

"Have you actually learned anything about him yet?" She asked, ignoring my comment.

"I think he might understand me, at least a little. Although, he doesn't seem to be able to talk," I told her, but I was not sure where she was going with this.

"Do you think he'll let us hunt in our own woods again?" She pressed.

"Well, he chased off a coyote last night and seemed pretty pissed that it was there." I leaned over to pick up my coffee as I took a sip and thought about how he'd communicated with me so far. Did I want to tell my sister about the interactions in detail?

"Have you asked this creature any yes or no questions?" She asked.

"Sort of. He pointed at my shotgun, and I asked him if he wanted to know if I was going to shoot him, but he shook his head no, so I figured he was asking about when I shot the Grunch head."

"Then tonight, we will go back to the dock together and see if he will agree to us hunting so we can do away with the boatman," she said as she got up and walked out of my room. I closed my eyes. Of course, this was about Clay. Something told me she would almost rather face Bigfoot alone than keep using Clay's services. I finished my coffee and got dressed, uncertain about how to talk to my sisters yet. Theia seemed worried that I was putting myself in danger, while Ella wanted to use my talking to Sasquatch as an advantage.

When I walked out of my room, Theia was cooking breakfast. "About time you came out of hiding. What did Ella have to say to you?"

"She wants me to ask permission to hunt here again tonight," I told her, knowing it would piss her off.

"Why am I the only one who thinks talking to the Swamp Ape is a bad idea?" She asked as she dumped a pile of eggs onto a plate.

"I didn't say I was looking for him to talk to, you know. I went out there the other night like I normally do, and he just showed up. I ended up talking to him, just to see if he was capable of any sort of communication."

"So why did you go back last night? Were you looking for him?" She pressed as she plated the sausage.

"Not really; I was just trying to get my head out of the past," I admitted.

She looked at her palm, her eyes haunted with more pain than anyone should ever bear, and then she made a fist. "I can't blame you for wanting a distraction from Atlantis. I wish it could be wiped from our memories like it was from existence." She turned to the toaster, pulled the bread out, and placed it on our plates before taking her own and walking out the door to the front porch. I picked up mine and Ella's plates and followed her. We ate in silence before heading to the docks to meet Clay.

"You and your sisters have quite a home if you ever need any help keeping up with it. I'm pretty handy." Clay said as I boarded the boat. My sisters were not far behind me

"Are you saying our manor looks ill-kept?" I countered as I glanced back over at the mansion.

"Not at all; I'm just looking for a free meal in trade for some free labor," he said with a smile.

I shook my head. "I'm not so sure my sisters would like that. The three of us are very independent."

"Three delicate-looking ladies in boots, packing shotguns and machetes, independent?" He asked in a sarcastic but playful tone.

I couldn't help but smile. "Do you take anything seriously?"

"Would you still like me if I did?" He asked with a smile.

"I never said I liked you," I immediately defended.

He shrugged. "Your loss. I make a really good friend to just sit and talk to."

"Don't let her lie to you; she likes you. Ella doesn't, but she hates all men," Theia said as she got onto the boat, having heard the last of the conversation. Ella rolled her eyes and boarded without saying a word.

"Theia," I hissed under my breath.

Clay chuckled. "Is the jury still out with you?" He asked Theia.

She tilted her head and looked at him. "You piss my sister off, and I might feel a little sad about cutting your head off. Both of them," she added as she turned around and sat down, waiting to leave the dock.

"I do my best not to anger my employers," he said casually, not realizing how deadly serious my sister was. He leaned over toward me and added. "When you decide you want to talk to me as a friend, just know my social skills are rusty. I spend most of my time in the swamp, so we might end up laughing about frog legs and gator bits."

"Shut up and take us to a good hunting spot," I said as I sat down, doing my best to hide my blush.

Half an hour later, Clay stopped the boat close to shore, and my sisters and I headed into the swamp. Hours later, yet another hunting trip with no coypu left my sisters and me packing a small boar back to the boat. Clay immediately stood up and placed his book down when he saw us coming. "I'll be! That's one hell of a catch! Let me get out of the way," he said as he moved some things around and quickly spread out a tarp.

"Should be good eating," I said as we packed it onto the boat.

"Not a bad size either! Y'all got a roaster?" He asked.

"Yep," I said, settling the boar onto the tarp.

He leaned around me and tossed the tarp over the boar. "Don't want the flies getting at it before we get back." He shoved a cooler over to us. "I got some bottled water in there if y'all need or want it. That was a heavy kill to pack in."

"Thanks," I said, opening the cooler, taking a bottle out, and offering it to Theia.

She frowned. "Thanks." I knew better than to hand a bottle to Ella. She'd rather die than accept anything from a male. While Theia was a little more accepting of Clay, she still held trust issues for anyone other than Ella or me.

We pulled up to the dock, and I tugged the tarp back off the boar while Theia and Ella grabbed its feet and began to pack it off the boat. "Remember what I said about free labor for free food," Clay said to me with a wink. "I would put in an awful lot of free labor for some smoked hog."

Theia glanced back as Clay, and I folded up his tarp. "Get your own boar, boatman," she tossed over her shoulder before looking back in the direction they were headed with the boar.

I sighed, "My sisters really don't socialize well."

"No need to explain things. You warned me when you hired me for this job," he said before stopping and just looking at me.

"What? Do I have something on my face?" I asked, feeling awkward.

"No, sorry for staring like that, but you are captivating, you know that? Beautiful without even trying."

"Clay-" I said, trying to cut him off.

"The more I get to know you, the more I like you," he finished.

"Clay, I'm not looking for anything but a way into the swamp for my sisters and me," I told him, hating that I wanted nothing more than to jump his bones, stupid itch!

"I know Kassie. I just had to tell you. You've not given me any signs of interest, but I wanted you to know that if you ever do find me interesting, I'm right here, and I'd never hurt you."

I swallowed hard, "I think you should go now."

"Sure thing; I'll see you in a couple of days for another hunting trip. Sorry if I made you feel uncomfortable. I won't let it happen again," he said with a smile.

"Right, well, be safe," I said, feeling stupid as I got off the boat and walked towards my sisters without looking back.

"Boatman has a thing for you," Theia said as I approached them.

"Shut up," I snapped.

"Might help with the nightmares if you get rid of that itch, just saying," Theia continued.

"I said shut up," I warned.

"I mean, after we check with Bigfoot tonight, we may not need his services anymore, and you can just feel free to have him satisfy your needs?" Theia pressed.

Without hesitation, I launched myself at her, tackling her to the ground and punching her in the face. "Shut up!" I yelled as I drew back to punch her again.

She kicked me off of her. "All this aggression could be taken care of!" She yelled, pointing in the direction of the dock. "He's right there."

"I don't want to get hurt again!" I yelled at her, ducking her blow and punching her in the side of the knee, dropping her.

"Pussy!" She spat and launched herself at me, recovering quickly. Pain seared through my shoulder and collarbone as her punch landed just above my left breast. Her other fist connected with my chin, and I staggered back, the metallic taste of blood filling my mouth. I let out a roar of rage and charged her, knocking her to the ground again.

We rolled around in the dirt, trading punches and insults, taking our aggression over the itch out on one another. Ella quietly processed the boar as if we were invisible, bleeding and screaming at each other in the dirt.

When we both sprawled into the dirt, gasping for breath, Theia smiled weakly at me, "Thanks for not knocking out my teeth."

"Thanks for not biting me," I said as I offered her my hand to help her to her feet.

"You know I'm right, though," she said once she was on her feet.

"Are you *really* trying to start this again?" I asked with narrowed eyes.

"I'm done now," she said as she turned and looked at Ella. "We'll clean up the scraps."

"Damn, straight you will. I'm not cooking it either," Ella said as she glanced at us. "Go clean yourselves up, get out here, and finish the job."

Theia and I went into the house and cleaned up from our fight, then went back out and finished processing the boar, prepped it, and began the slow job of roasting it over the next twelve hours. After eating dinner, we headed out to the dock to see if Bigfoot would show up. We sat on the dock for twenty minutes before Ella glared in my direction. "How long do you normally wait for him to show up?"

"I've only seen him here twice; it's not like we have a standard meeting time or anything," I snapped at her, not liking her tone.

"Show yourself, Sasquatch!" She yelled into the darkness.

"That's a great idea. – just anger the powerful Swamp Ape," Theia muttered next to me.

A low growl sounded in the darkness across the water. "Great, you pissed him off," I muttered. Bigfoot stepped out of the trees, his eyes locked on my face, then turned to look at Theia, his eyes roaming over her, before finally setting on Ella. He roared in her direction, but she didn't even flinch. "Yep, he's pissed at you."

"Now that I have your attention, fur ball, do you think you could let us hunt the swamp again?" Ella demanded, ignoring my comment. He bared his teeth at her and pointed at me. Ella turned and arched a brow at me, "Am I talking to It wrong?"

I pinched my nose and winced in pain, having forgotten about the cut across it from my earlier fight with Theia. "Hey, Big Fella, can we hunt this swamp or not?"

He let out a snarl, touched his face, and gestured to me again. "I think he wants to know what happened to your face," Theia said in a confused tone.

"I hit Theia because she told me to jump the boatman, and we ended up in a full-blown fistfight; now can we hunt or not?" I demanded. He made a strange scoffing sound as though he were laughing then shook his head no.

"Why not?" Ella demanded. Bigfoot roared at her in response and pointed at me, then his face. "He doesn't fucking understand," Ella jumped off the dock and stood in waist-deep water. "Can we hunt this swamp and get rid of the damn boatman?" She grated out. He stomped into the water and roared at her, then slammed his hand at the surface of the water, splashing her. Her shoulders tensed, and she let out a yell of frustration.

"I think that's a no," I said, crossing my arms. "We will ask again in a few days."

"Dumb Swamp Ape," Ella yelled. Bigfoot snorted and walked out of the water.

<u>Chapter 8</u>

Twelve thousand years ago…

 I walked a step behind the queen in silence; this wasn't the first time she'd done this. She wanted me to evaluate the guards with her. She had me test any new guards and had several of them. The first time had been horrifying as were the few times that had followed. But I had been her servant for a few years and I had grown accustomed to it. We, her beautiful servants, were the buffer between her and the king. As far as he knew, her depravity only went as far as watching us with the guards. Should he discover the truth, she would perish as would all those involved.

"Tell me, what do you think of that one?" She asked with a slight nod to a guard.

I considered his features carefully. He didn't look particularly cruel, not like some of the others. "He looks strong enough, I suppose. He is a guard, though; he should have the stamina."

The queen snorted, "I would have thought you knew better than that by now. Just because they can hold their sword in hand doesn't mean they aren't quick to finish the ... battle."

"Yes, My Queen. I suppose I should say he doesn't look like the type to rush for his own sake."

"There, that is what I've been training you for." She turned and smiled at me. "Shall we test him or keep looking for a while?"

"I shall follow your lead, as always, My Queen." I'd told her once I didn't want to test them. She'd pouted, looking remorseful, and ordered that very guard to strip me bare and slap my backside until I cried. When he'd finished with that, and tears had streamed down my face, she'd ordered him to slap between my thighs until I admitted I *wanted to test him for her. It wasn't until after she'd watched him slap*

and rub between my legs at her command four or five times that she'd

told me how to make it all end. All I had to do was agree to test her

newest lover while she watched and evaluated his performance.

She hummed and smiled at me. "One more walk through the

halls, and I may give you another to consider. I want to see if you have a

good eye for those well suited to my requirements." Nodding my head in

silent agreement, we began walking again. It was an hour later, and

three guards she'd given me to choose from when she finally sighed and

leaned against one of the sandstone arches looking out over the

gardens. "Tell me which one was your least favorite."

I thought for a moment, letting the sea breeze cool my face as I

listened to the galls. "The second one."

"Why? I found them all equally pleasing to look at, didn't

you?"

Bowing my head, I looked at her from under my lashes. "You

always select males who are pleasing to look at, but it is my job to try to

see if that is all they have to offer, My Queen. The second, while

handsome, didn't look," I paused, glancing away from her as I thought of how to phrase it. "The second looked like a rabbit, while the other two looked like lions."

The corner of her mouth tilted in a near smile. "I do enjoy the way you think. Explain why I should prefer a lion over a rabbit."

"Rabbits are soft and fast, darting for the finish line and only nibbling their food. Lions take their time to hunt down their meal. Lions feast, fully enjoying what they eat." As I said this, my cheeks filled with heat and the queen's half-smile grew into a full, heated grin.

"You are my favorite servant." She stepped away from where she leaned. "We will test them both." She turned and began walking in the direction of the first guard. "Guards are meant to work together as a unit, after all. Why not see how well they can work together?"

*"You mean, you want me to test them both at the same time?" I nearly choked on the question. She could have me whipped or strapped down while **they** tested **me** if she thought I was refusing.*

She stopped and half turned to me, her kohl-lined eyes narrowing. "Do you disagree?"

My eyes widened, and I quickly lowered my head. "No, My Queen, I'm just nervous. I fear disappointing you."

"Sweet Kassandra, I'm not worried about you disappointing me, but them. That's why I'm having you test them for me."

"Yes, My Queen."

"All you have to do is what I tell you I would do. I'll be there, as usual, guiding you. After all, what good would it do me to not see with my own eyes how they perform?"

"I would not lie about them to you, but I am grateful for your presence, ensuring we all do as you wish."

She sighed. "I am quite kind to you. You are very fortunate that I chose you to be my servant instead of selling you to another kingdom." She turned then, her lavender dress with its gold pins swishing softly with her movements.

"I can't express my gratitude enough, My Queen," the words came out almost automatically as I followed her again down the breezy outer hall of the castle.

We walked in silence until we reached the guard in question. The queen gave a coy smile, slightly tilting her regal head to the side, her eyes roaming over the guard in open appreciation. Her dark head turned to me, then back to the guard. "Tell me, do you find us both attractive?"

The guard openly looked us both over, his eyes catching on our breasts, hips, and lips. "You are each very beautiful, My Queen. The king is lucky to have such a beauty as you for his wife."

"The King is lucky indeed. Servant, do you find him agreeable?"

"Yes, My Queen. He is most definitely agreeable," I confirmed, mimicking her coy grin as I looked at the male who would be joining me within her private chambers soon enough. I'd found that, while I didn't entirely enjoy her watching or picking the males I shared my body with, it was easier to handle if I engaged agreeably with it all.

"Tell me, have you ever shared a woman?" The queen asked the guard.

His eyes widened as he looked between the two of us, and he swallowed. "Shared, how, My Queen?"

She shrugged, her beautiful face tilting away from the guard. "With another man," she paused and glanced at me before continuing, "or another woman, in pleasure?"

He glanced around before looking back at us. "I have not, but it sounds rather intriguing. Do you have plans for me, My Queen?"

"Come with us and find out," she said before turning and walking in the direction of the hall where the other guard she'd chosen was stationed. The queen quickly seduced the second guard, and we returned to her private chambers. The queen led us into her room, which held a seat with overstuffed pillows, her dressing table and mirror, a large bed, and an intricate rug at the foot of that large bed. "Kassandra, help them to get comfortable." She reclined back on her seat and plucked a grape from her bowl.

Aware of the queen's eyes on me and the display she wanted, I sauntered up to the first guard, running my hand down the front of him to his belt that held his sword. "You won't be needing this in here." I removed the belt and sword with practiced hands, dropping them on the floor carelessly before turning my eyes to the other guard. "You won't be needing your capes or your armor either." Their leather armor slapped against the floor as it dropped.

"Stop." The queen's voice was soft and husky yet still laced with authority. "I changed my mind. Let them undress themselves, then you may inspect them."

I took a few steps, still facing the guards. I watched as they finished undressing, pulling their tunics over their heads and stripping down to nothing. Their erections bobbed in front of me, two males at one time. Hesitantly, I edged forward, circling each of them, trailing my fingers over their chests, arms, and backs. "Do they please your eyes, My Queen?"

"My eyes are indeed pleased, as are theirs, I believe," she purred from her seat. As I made my way back around to the front of them, I turned and looked over my shoulder at the queen. "Tell me how they feel in your soft hands." She reached up and pulled the golden pins holding her dress over her breasts.

"Yes, My Queen." I turned back to the males before me, put a hand on each man's stomach, and leaned slightly left as that hand slid down to cup his balls. The guard shuddered and grasped my wrist as though he would hold my hand there. "He's heavy, My Queen. Ready for what we have planned." I trailed a finger up the length of him, earning a twitch and a hitch in his breathing. I leaned to the other side and slid my hand down to cup the other male's balls; he gave a pleased shudder. "Oh yes, they are both heavy with desire for you, My Queen."

"For us," she corrected, the sound of her gold belt hitting the floor echoing from the stone walls. Behind me, I knew she was completely disrobed now. *"Which one of you thinks my servant is overdressed?"*

"Will you be joining us, My Queen?" the taller one asked, his reddish brown hair falling in his face as he stepped behind me. *"Or are we just to amuse you by pleasuring your servant?"* His hands grabbed my hips as he stepped right up against me, his erection brushing the cheeks of my ass through the thin dress I wore. He walked me forward a few steps until the other guard pulled the pins from my dress, the soft cotton dropping from my breast.

"I'll take my time to decide." The queen's voice came from behind me.

The male behind me brushed his lips against my bare shoulder, his hands sliding up to cup my breasts. *"Remove her belt; our queen is right. She's overdressed,"* he said to the other guard, whose dark eyes flashed toward my breasts and then to the queen. I, too, looked at the queen. She leaned back in her seat, her legs spread and her hands roaming her body.

"What shall they do to me, My Queen?" My body was heating. Part of me liked the humiliation of being watched, I supposed. Knowing her hazel eyes were as focused on our bodies.

"They will make you moan, my golden treasure, and you will tell me how one of them tastes while the other tells me how you taste."

"Will you not taste all of us yourself," the dark-eyed guard said boldly as his hand cupped between my legs. "She's wet already, My Queen."

"Clever man," the queen said in a breathy voice.

The male behind me nipped my ear, his erection rubbing gently against the cheeks of my now-naked ass, the removal of the belt having let it fall the rest of the way from my body. "Has the queen already tasted you? Is that why she's content to watch as we taste you? As you taste us?"

"It's not wise to ask about what goes on in the queen's chambers," I said as I rolled my head back to allow him better access, one hand in his hair, the other reaching out to grip the erection in front of me.

"Kneel on the bed for them," the queen demanded. They stepped away from me and I walked to the bed, climbing upon it only to have them follow me, one stayed behind me while the other remained in front. "Now, feast on one another, make her whimper with pleasure before you may seek your own, then switch."

"While her lips are on my cock, could mine not be on you, My Queen," that dark-eyed guard again made a bold request of my queen.

"Do you wonder what your queen tastes like? Am I sweet like the fruit in this bowl, or am I savory? When your tongue delves between my legs, will a robust flavor like that of a bold wine greet you? Will my golden treasure taste as sweet as she looks?" The queen teased him, her fingers slipping inside her wet pussy. I glanced at the guard as I sat on the bed, waiting to see how this would play out. "I have an idea." The queen rose from where she was sitting.

"You," she pointed at the guard who'd been behind me, "you are going to lay down on the bed, while my sweet Kassandra will spread her legs over your face and wrap her lips around his cock," she pointed at the other one, still looking at the first man, "while you bury yourself deep inside me."

The dark-haired guard laid down on the bed, the dark-eyed one, and smiled devilishly. I readjusted, my knees on either side of his face, leaning forward onto my hands. His hands gripped my thighs as his hot breath teased my pussy. The dark-eyed male was on the bed in front of me. My arms quivered, and my eyes went to his erection. I licked my lips and felt the shifting of weight on the bed as the queen mounted the *guard whose face was between my thighs, his tongue darting out and*

flicking against my sensitive flesh, teasing but not slipping between my

wet folds. He groaned before his lips latched onto the bundle of nerves,

the cock in front of me slipping between my parted lips with a slow push

of his hips. The queen's hands came forward, her nails dragging gently

over my back as she rode the male beneath us, and I sucked the one in

front, dark eyes reaching forward to touch the queen.

The four of us traded positions for hours—each of us tasting the

other. Moans, demands, grunts, groans, and the smacking and slurping

of bare flesh bounced off the walls of the queen's chambers. When the

guards had reached their climax, their cocks shrinking back with their

release, the queen demanded they each take turns feasting on us until

they grew hard again. Sweat slicked our bodies, the musty smell of our

orgy filling the room.

I woke with a start, a half moan on my lips, my heart pounding like mad in my ears. The dream of that first time sharing two males with the queen had been vivid. "Fuck." I said as I dragged my hands through my hair. I needed a shower and a good lay. Damn, itch. At least this dream had not been a nightmare.

Chapter 9

Kassie…

The smell of roasted hog filled the manor, but as Theia and I got in the old truck, we were assaulted by the stench of rotting garbage. It was time for our drive to the dump. Ella was the lucky one this time who got to stay at the manor and take care of things there while Theia and I loaded and unloaded the truck bed full of nasty. The smell was putrid even in the truck's cab in the Louisiana heat. I rolled down the passenger window and closed my eyes, accepting my smelly fate as my exhaustion from last night weighed on me.

When the truck came to a stop, I opened my eyes, ready to get out and start throwing bags into the compactor, only to find that we were at the boat docks in town. "What the hell are we doing here?" I asked, turning an accusing glare at Theia.

"I'm going to pay the boatman to unload the trash," she said with a smile, then hopped out of the truck.

"Theia! Theia, get back here!" Some passers-by slowed down and looked at me. I felt myself turn bright red and sunk in the seat. "I'm going to kill her," I muttered to myself. Glancing out the window, I wondered if Clay was even working today. With a growl of frustration, I sat up and flipped the visor down to look at myself. My battered and bruised face from last night was gone. My hair was hanging in a long, wavy mess and tucked behind my ears, with a hair elastic on my wrist. "Damn it, Theia!" I muttered and tried to pull my hair back in a decent ponytail. "Why do I even care?" I asked my reflection before slamming the visor shut again and crossing my arms as I waited on Theia.

"Do I ride on top of the trash?" Clay asked, making me jump. He smiled, "I didn't mean to startle you; it's just that I'm a little too big to fit in the middle."

"I'll scoot over," I said, sliding to the middle. Theia got in and smiled at me. "I'll deal with you later," I hissed.

"Climb on in, Clay; Kassie will be sure to pack you a big old plate of food for our next hunting trip," Theia said with a stubborn smile.

"When is that exactly?" Clay asked as he got in next to me, his hip and thigh pressing against mine.

"We won't need to hunt for at least another day or two, but if you require some sort of retainer, I'm sure we can figure something out if you come by the manor tomorrow morning," Theia offered without looking at him.

I was going to kill Theia if Ella didn't beat me to it. "If you have other customers, you should feel free to take them on. I'm sure we can find another way into the bayou if you're unavailable," I told him, glancing at him and then away.

"I'm available, Kassie," he said, then looked out the window. "What I mean to say is, there hasn't been much work at the docks. That's another reason I offered to help around y'alls manor."

"We do have all that wood that needs to be chopped up before winter," Theia offered.

"I think Ella is working on it right now," I said, scowling at my sister.

"Just admit it, Kassie, we need help around the place. It's falling apart, and the boatman has been keeping things professional."

"The boatman has a name," I grated each word out, feeling my cheeks flush as I glanced at Clay, who seemed to be suppressing a laugh. "You think this is funny?"

"My sister and I used to bicker like the two of you. I think you'd get along with her," he said, looking at me and never once at Theia.

I rolled my eyes. "You know Theia is meddling, don't you," I said accusingly.

"I'm not going to complain as long as I get some of that boar," he replied, his amber eyes twinkling with mischief. I turned away from him, the itch in my throat roaring with reinvigorated ferocity. "As far as work around the manor, I can help by pulling down some of those vines that are trying to overtake the place. I'm taller than the three of you, so I should be able to reach things y'all can't."

"Thanks, I'll keep that in mind," I said, wishing I could scoot further away from him.

Clay leaned over and whispered in my ear, "Your hair looks nice, by the way."

My eyes widened, and my cheeks flushed all over again. He'd seen me messing with it while I waited on them! "It's just a ponytail," I muttered sheepishly.

"I'm used to seeing it in a braid, is all." With that, he looked away from me and out the window again.

It was a ten-minute drive from the docks to the dump, but by the time we reached the wretched-smelling place, my throat was on fire. I climbed out of the driver's door and kicked Theia in the back of the calf, making her stagger. "Oh, Theia, you should *really* watch your step," I said in false concern as she caught herself on the truck.

She glared at me. "It runs in the family, Kassandra," she said, using my full name.

"I'm just glad you didn't get out on my side," Clay said as he grabbed a bag of trash with each hand.

"What's that supposed to mean?" Theia snapped, ever the defensive sister.

"It means she kicked you because you're trying to set us up, and the two of you aren't very sneaky about it," Clay said as he walked away.

"See what you did," I hissed at Theia, elbowing her in the ribs.

"Just shut up and help with the trash. It's not like he minds; he has a fucking thing for you," she hissed back, her elbow connecting with my ribs in a return assault.

I grabbed a couple of bags and started toward the compactor, only to have Clay step in front of me. "She means well; the two of you should maybe talk before you start fighting," he said, concern in his eyes.

"I can handle my own sister, thank you very much," I said as I stepped around him and tossed my bags into the compactor.

"Or maybe you've been stuck in that house with just the two of them for too long," Clay said as I walked back to the truck with him for more trash.

"What is that supposed to mean?" I demanded, feeling insulted.

"It means you should have dinner with me. You can vent about your sisters, and I can tell you about mine."

"I thought we talked about this yesterday," I said, giving him a weary glance as I grabbed two more trash bags.

He grabbed two as well. "About our annoying and meddlesome sisters?" He asked with a confused expression on his face.

"Clay, you know what I'm talking about," I said as I trailed after him.

"Oh! You mean when I told you how pretty you are, and you shot me down cold?"

"Basically," I said awkwardly, suddenly feeling very small compared to him.

"I wasn't asking you out on a date. I was asking you to go complain about family in a public setting over a meal. I'm a man. I'm almost always hungry." He flashed a grin as he tossed his bags.

"I think you should get out of the house. I'm getting sick of you sighing and flopping that damn book down on the coffee table when you finish it," Theia chimed in, reminding me that she was close enough to hear every word. She leaned her arms on the other side of the truck bed. "Oh, and boatman, if you try anything, I will cut you up, put you in these nice plastic bags, and toss you into that compactor with the rest of the trash."

"Just dinner and chit-chat, ma'am," Clay said with a smile, southern charm thick in his voice.

"What the hell happened to the man-hating sister I got in the truck with?" I asked, stunned she would even make such a suggestion.

"You don't hate men," she said with a smile. "He's also not completely annoying."

"But you are," I snapped.

"Kassie and Clay, sitting in a tree," she began, then laughed as she packed two more bags to the compactor.

"You ladies sure do have a lot of trash," Clay said as he grabbed more bags, out of the truck bed, which was only half empty.

"We try not to come to town unless we really have to," I told him.

"Lunch, at your boat dock tomorrow. You bring the boar and I'll bring whatever drinks you want."

I shook my head. "You're not going to let this go, are you?"

"You do owe me for helping with all this trash. It smells truly horrible," he said, making a face as he picked up another bag.

I contemplated momentarily before sighing heavily, "Fine. Bring beer."

"Where's your sense of adventure? No shine?" He mused.

"You mean that crap they sell in the store? No thanks."

"Kassandra, darling, you wound this humble boatman with your cruel words! I would never offer that fake shit to anyone," he said with dramatic inflection.

Shaking my head, I smiled, "Fine, you get the real stuff, and I'm game."

We finished unloading the trash and drove Clay back to the docks, "See you tomorrow at 11:30. I like chipotle barbeque, just so you know," Clay said as he shut the door.

"Bring it yourself, then," I quipped back as I scooted over into the passenger seat. He smiled before walking away.

"That went well," Theia said with a faint smile tugging at the corners of her face.

"I'm going to fucking kill you," I seethed in my seat as she pulled onto the road.

"Just scratch your itch already, and you won't be so hostile," she said in a teasing tone.

"You do realize that he's going to be spending more time at the manor, around you and Ella, thanks to this little plan of yours?" I asked, wondering if she had considered the consequences of her little setup.

"Yeah, but he honestly doesn't seem to give a damn about me or Ella. I'm pretty sure he's had a thing for you from the start. He's a bloodhound who's got your scent, dear sister."

"Really, Theia," I exclaimed in exasperation. "A bloodhound on a scent? That's how you're looking at it?"

She chuckled. "Yep. All males are dogs; this one just happens to be the kind that trees the critter it's after."

"So I'm a fucking critter now?" I demanded a mix between amusement and annoyance.

"Aren't we all?" She asked with a smile as she glanced at me.

"Just keep your eyes on the road," I said, smiling in return.

"I know you don't want to get hurt again, but I also know how hard it is for you to be intimate with someone you don't have feelings for. You like him, and he likes you; get it over with and then end things before you get too attached," she said in a more serious tone.

Looking out the window, I took a moment to think about what she'd said. "The problem is, I'm afraid I'll care about him once I'm intimate with him. It's what always seems to happen. It's why I hate what we are."

"I know, Ella and I feel the same way. Look what happened the last time Ella cared about someone other than us?"

I turned a sad smile toward my sister. "The war was fun, though."

Theia shook her head. "We are sick individuals."

"We are creatures of myth and legend. We're supposed to be messed up," I told her as I looked out the window. Part of me loved violence, and the other part of me hated it. Simply being happy had never really been an option for us, though. We had to fight to survive, and every victory came with a sweet rush of satisfaction and self-appreciation. When we battled, we weren't slaves to the itch any longer; we were free, fluid, and deadly. Even if every battle pleased our cock sucker father.

"What I don't understand is why your itch is so bad. You've used your power a few times now; it should have curved it a little, even without physical satisfaction," Theia said after a few minutes, interrupting my thoughts.

"I've been thinking the same thing. I'm not sure what's changed. I've always been able to keep myself under control if I just scratch the surface of it, but I lost it yesterday. I'm sorry," I said without looking at her.

"I needed the release, and part of me knew you were an easy trigger. I would apologize, but we both needed it," she admitted.

She didn't realize I'd not found the release I normally did when we fought. I was still a ball of tension, the itch in my throat driving me crazy that being near Clay today had been almost physically painful. "I did need it," I told her, leaving it at that. Clay was coming for lunch, and I wasn't so sure I'd be able to handle it. While I believed he wouldn't press his attraction to me, I wasn't sure I could contain mine.

<u>Chapter 10</u>

Kassie...

Ella had taken the news of Clay helping around the manor as I'd expected– badly. My sisters ended up in another physical fight while I sat on the porch and watched them trade punches and kicks on the moss-covered lawn. The itch in my throat roared as I watched them. The physical exertion of a fight may have helped, but I couldn't risk not healing in time with Clay coming by tomorrow.

That night, Ella still wasn't speaking to Theia or myself. Theia and I knew it would be a few days before she would get over it. Theia sat on the couch with her busted-up, but rapidly healing face and played online with a particularly enthusiastic bloodlust. I pulled out my tequila and walked down to the dock with the shotgun and bottle in hand. When I arrived, Bigfoot was already on the other side of the water, sprawled on his back and looking up at the sky. When he heard me approach, he sat up on an elbow and looked me over before laying back down, his massive arms behind his head.

"Getting used to my company?" I asked in amusement as I sat on the end of the dock. He put his hand on his mouth and gestured for me to sing the way he had that first night. "Oh, I see, you just like a night-time lullaby." He snorted in response but didn't look at me. "Alright, I'll sing just one song, but then you get to listen as I tell you about my day." With that, I started singing a song that was long forgotten by society, one I'd learned in Egypt thousands of years ago. A song I'd learned before we helped King Narmer defeat Lower Egypt.

As I finished singing my song, Bigfoot sat up and rested his back against a tree as if he were ready to listen to what I had to say. "Alright, well. Today, Theia and I took off our trash, which was a lot because we really don't like going to town. As you'd imagine, going to town can be dangerous for us. What I didn't know was that Theia used it as an excuse to set me up with Clay, our boatman. He's nice and handsome, but I don't want to get close to him. I can't get close to anyone. The last time I got close to someone, the mob killed him. I got my revenge. Jimmy's body will never be found, but that doesn't change the fact that every time I get close to someone they die, violently," probably because of our father I mentally chimed in, but Bigfoot didn't need to know that.

As the pain of the memory washed over me, I stared absently at my knees. I looked back up at Bigfoot, who was still watching me, perhaps waiting for me to continue. "I didn't love him. In all my centuries, I've only loved one male. When Naoki was taken from me, I built walls around my heart. That doesn't mean I haven't cared deeply for anyone, though. I wish it did." I laid my back against the post and looked up at the stars. "I can't tell Clay any of this. I don't know why it bothers me so bad that I can't. After twelve thousand years, I shouldn't be able to feel anymore. I've watched so many mortals fade from existence without so much as a gravestone to mark their death."

I looked back at Bigfoot and noticed he was looking at me with his deep amber eyes, and his expression seemed saddened. I offered him a smile, "I get the feeling you understand at least a little of my pain.

Have you ever lost a lover?" He shook his head no. "Are you the only one of your kind?" I asked, feeling as though I'd been inconsiderate. He shook his head no again. "I guess I shouldn't keep asking you questions; your kind is as much a mystery in the immortal community as it is in the human one," I said with a smile.

To my surprise, he shrugged. I tilted my head and looked at him for a moment. "Have you ever done this before? Sat with someone who wasn't your kind and just talked?" He shook his head, no, and I smiled. "I'm flattered to be the exception. Even if you don't talk back, talking to you is nice. Part of that might be that my sisters talk back too quickly; sometimes they don't give me a chance to really feel. I know they don't mean to be that way, but we're sisters. I see that kind of behavior with human siblings as well. I guess that's why Clay offered to talk to me about his sister." A mosquito landed on my arm, and I looked at it, just sitting there. They fed off of every mortal being I knew of but not us. "Do mosquitos bother you?" I asked, suddenly curious.

He snorted and shook his head in the negative. Rolling my eyes, I smiled at him. "They don't bother me either. I guess that means you're immortal, too?" He nodded in agreement. "Is that why you aren't afraid of the gun?" I asked, wondering if a Bigfoot could be killed at all. He narrowed his eyes and shook his head no. "I'm not trying to find a way to kill you; I'm just wondering if you trust me without any real reason to," I elaborated, suddenly feeling nervous.

He made a fist and tapped it against his chest over his heart. "I guess you are trying to say you trust me?" He nodded his head. "I guess I kinda trust you too. I will miss you when we move on from these parts," I said as I leaned my head back again, gazing at the stars. "We have a few years left before humans will start to notice we aren't aging. I hope you stick around for that long." I looked over at him then to see the sad expression on his ape-like face again. "Will you miss me when we leave?" He bared his teeth at me then, shocking me. I sat up and blinked at him, "Are you telling me to leave?" He shook his head in the negative, and I thought for a moment, trying to figure out why he'd growled at me.

"Are you telling me not to leave?" I finally asked. He nodded his head, causing a pang of sympathy in my chest. "Oh, big fella, it doesn't work that way for us. We have to stay hidden from everyone, humans and immortals alike. I'll make you a deal, though. I'll tell you where we plan to go, and you can come visit; maybe you and Ella can even learn to get along." He snorted and made me laugh. "You've hardly encountered her, yet, you already seem to know her so well." I shook my head and then glanced at the manor. "It's getting late; I'd better go in before Theia comes out to get me. She *really* doesn't trust you." He shrugged, then leaned back against the tree as if to say he didn't care.

Getting up, I took a drink of the tequila and headed back to the manor. Frogs sang around me as I walked across the soft, mossy ground. Looking down at the bottle in my hand as I walked, I decided it wasn't worth getting drunk tonight. The burn of the tequila was a nice distraction from the itch in my throat, but tonight, I wanted the sounds of the bayou to lull me to sleep instead of the fog of alcohol.

Walking into the kitchen door, I turned to the right and put the bottle in the freezer for the night. I walked into the living room, where Theia was loading a new mission. She looked up at me with a judgmental expression. "Been talking to the Swamp Ape again?"

"He sends his love to you and Ella," I told her as I sat beside her. She rolled her eyes. "The tequila isn't cutting it tonight," I admitted as I twisted around on the couch and laid my head in her lap.

"Thinking about the past again?" She asked, stroking my hair.

"Yeah. About Detroit," I admitted.

"That was what, '75?" She asked, her beautiful face and dark-lined lashes reflecting her thoughtfulness. The soft glow of the television cast a warm hue on her features.

"Yeah," I confirmed.

"They are still looking for Hoffa's remains, you know. It was nice of the mafia to let us use the incinerator," she said thoughtfully, her tongue playing with her lip ring from the inside.

"As if they had a choice. At least his wife was free of him after that," I told her. I could still hear the metal of the car crushing in as it collided with the tree. Hoffa had thought I was dead, too, but instead, it was just my lover. I'd told Ronny not to get involved with them, but he hadn't listened. The human justice system had proven that they were useless when they let him go. Had I not been involved with Ronny, it wouldn't have mattered to me. "I've made so many mistakes, yet it feels like I just keep repeating the same ones."

"We all do. It's the price we pay for being immortal," she said, her headset muted as her team began their mission. "I need to focus now. Is that okay?" She asked, glancing down at me.

"As long as it's okay for me to keep laying here for a little while," I said, turning to watch her game. I fell asleep there, just listening and watching her play. Sometime in the middle of the night, she woke me up, and I went to bed, sleeping nude because I was too tired to put on my PJs. My dreams were filled with the sound of shattered glass and gunshots. When I woke up, my mind was still on that back country road from 1975. I got dressed and made my way barefoot over the wooden floors in the kitchen, where I splashed whiskey into my coffee instead of my regular milk.

The screen door creaked as I opened it and walked onto the front porch to join Ella. After giving me an angry look, she stood up and walked towards the barn with determination. I sighed, went to one of the wooden rocking chairs, and sat down. She would be pissed for days. Theia came around the side of the house and sat in the chair next to me. "Glad the bitch is gone. You know she threw a knife at me this morning when I came out?"

I nearly choked on my coffee, laughing. "Sounds like Ella. Good thing she's a good aim, or she may have *actually* hit you."

"She shattered my coffee mug!" Theia exclaimed while glaring at the scattered, broken pieces on the floor.

I shrugged. "Well, you did do the one thing that can piss her off the most, you invited a male over without a legitimate cause."

"Your itch and stubbornness is a legitimate cause. You don't say it, but the discomfort is written all over your face, not to mention you rub your throat a lot recently."

"Great," I said, my voice laced with a hint of irritation, taking a drink of my spiked coffee.

"I can also smell the whiskey in your mug. You should use mouthwash before Clay gets here, or the boatman will think you're a lush," she said as she looked out at the bayou and drank her new mug of coffee.

"He's bringing me genuine moonshine. I believe the lush ship has already sailed," I informed her.

"Tell me he's bringing enough for all of us!" She exclaimed eagerly.

"I don't think he's bringing a couple of gallons of it. The stuff isn't easy for mortals to get a hold of; he'll probably only bring a quart," I said, looking at her.

She asked me excitedly, her body humming with energy, "Hey after you're done with your date, do you think we could get him to clean out the gutters?"

Looking at her in exasperation, I asked, "What is wrong with you?"

"I don't like the smell of rotting leaves; you can't fault me for that," she countered. I just shook my head. "If he's here, he might as well do something I don't want to do." We drank the rest of our coffee in silence before going about the rest of our morning chores. Ella didn't come out of the barn except to get a bottle of water and a plate of food. The sounds of her hitting the punching bag in anger resounded from inside the manor. I wondered if she would forgive Theia or me first, as she blamed us both.

At eleven, I went into the house and got lunch ready for Clay and me. I was torn between being almost excited to see him and pissed that Theia had manipulated the situation. At twenty past eleven, I walked down to the dock and waited for Clay. Within five minutes, his fan boat was coming down the waterway. As he got closer to the dock, he tied off just a few feet from where I was standing. "Morning Kassie, I hope you don't mind that I brought two jars of shine, one for us and one for your sisters. I figured Ella would be pissed that I'm here, seeing as she seems to hate my existence."

I smiled and laughed. "Don't take it personally; she's like that with everyone; either doesn't acknowledge or hates you."

"But I'd bet she'd kill for you and Theia," he said as he got off the boat and handed me a jar.

"You have no idea," I replied.

"Oh, I think I do. If someone hurt my little sister, the gators would eat well," he said with a seriousness that I believed.

"How many siblings do you have?" I asked curiously.

"Just the one. She doesn't live here, though. We call and chat every now and then and get together for the holidays." He sat down next to me and smiled. "When we were kids, we'd fuss and argue the way you and your sisters do. Makes me miss her."

"What's her name?" I asked, not sure how to make conversation with him.

"Maggie. She's tall for a girl, almost as tall as I am. We have the same hair and eyes, but we're full siblings," he told me as if it explained things.

"My sisters and I are triplets. I'm not sure why we look so different," I admitted. Even among immortals, siblings tended to look alike.

"I suppose stranger things have happened. Cats can have litters of kittens, and not a single one looks the same. Not that you remind me of cats." He closed his eyes and looked at his hands before looking back up at me with a half smile. "I told you I wasn't good at being social. You ask me a question about the bayou, and I can tell you just about anything without hesitation, but you ask me to make normal conversation, and I'm going to put my foot in my mouth."

"Don't worry, I'm not much better. My interactions consist of Ella, whose passion is weapons, and Theia, who's always doing online gaming, normally black ops and things like that," I assured him.

"So you read books in order to get away from it all," he said in a knowing tone.

"Exactly. Traveling isn't exactly easy. We don't interact well," I explained.

"So tell me what you thought of the book I gave you. Have you finished it?" He asked, latching onto the subject.

I laughed. "You only just gave it to me! In case you forgot, we had a boar to process and cook. You're eating that boar right now."

"It's very good, too," he said with a grin. "Alright, tell me about your favorite book, and I'll tell you about mine."

"I've read a lot of books; I don't know that I have a favorite," I said, smiling before taking a drink of the shine.

He chuckled before saying, "My kind of woman, takes a drink of homebrew without even flinching!"

"I live in the bayou; it takes more than a sip of shine to make me flinch," I said with a wink. He chuckled again, and I asked, "Alright, do you have a favorite book?"

"Not really," he said with a sheepish grin. "I was just trying to make conversation. Seeing as how you're a bayou girl, though, how about your most exciting hunt?"

Looking at him, I took another drink of the shine. "Well, right before we contracted you, we were hunting this area. It was a normal hunt, trudging through the swamp in our boots, packing our weapons and stuff when something big came barreling through the trees. It was like nothing we'd ever heard or seen before. At first, we thought it might be a bear, but when it got close to us, it wasn't a bear."

He smiled, "Ah, you encountered a swamp creature of some sort?"

"I knew you wouldn't believe me." I smiled at him.

"Folks see all kinds of strange things in the bayou. The question is, did you get a good look at the thing to know what kind of creature it was?"

"It was probably a sick bear covered in foliage, and my sisters and I were hot and freaked out," I said with a shrug. "Though, it sounds more exciting to say that it was a swamp monster, doesn't it?"

He laughed. "It sure does. Just like me saying I was out gator hunting one night and ran into a Grunch instead. It's probably nothing more than the imagination playing tricks on weary eyes." We laughed and talked like that for another hour before cleaning up the lunch. "Let me help you take it all in to wash," he said as he held onto his plate.

"I can manage just fine. I do believe Theia wanted to have you clean the gutters, though," I told him as I tugged on his plate.

He smiled down at me. "Do I have to guess where to find your sister and a ladder, or are you going to tell me?"

Chewing on my bottom lip, I remembered the ladder was in the barn where Ella was lurking. He shocked me when he reached forward and cupped my face. "What are you doing?" I asked, frozen in place.

"Pulling you out of whatever thought you were lost in. If you have work for me, I'm glad to do it," he said, dropping his hand.

"I think you should go," I said, feeling the itch in my throat rearing its ugly head again.

"If that's what you want. I was really hoping you'd say I should kiss you, but it's way too soon in our not-a-relationship," he said with a sad smile.

"It's never a good idea to mix business with pleasure," I told him, still not moving away. The damn itch in my throat had me anchored in place. It insisted that a handsome male was standing right there, ready to satisfy my every desire. *What would it feel like to have him pounding between my legs while his tongue plunged in and out of my mouth?*

"Very wise indeed," he said before leaning forward and placing a kiss on my cheek. "Sorry, I couldn't resist. When you need me, I'll be at the docks in town," he said before returning to his boat.

Chapter 11

Kassie…

I stood there and watched his boat pull away and move down the waterway like an idiot. He glanced back at me and smiled a half-hearted smile one time before focusing on maneuvering the bend that would take him out of sight. Turning towards the house, I let out a frustrated sigh and picked up the plates, intentionally leaving the two jars of moonshine on the dock. I reached the manor, Theia opened the kitchen door and glared at me. "What the hell? I wasn't joking about him cleaning the gutters."

Rolling my eyes, I shouldered by her and into the kitchen. "Stop complaining and go down to the dock and grab the two jars of shine, would you?"

"Ohhh! I knew he wasn't all bad for a male," she said happily, her gutter complaint forgotten. I was almost done with the dishes when she returned and put the unopened jar of shine in the fridge before leaning against the counter and looking at me. "So why did the boatman leave so soon?"

"Because you shouldn't mix business with pleasure, and he knows it," I told her as I dried and put away the plates.

"So don't get busy with it on his boat, and it's all good," she said with a wiggle of her brows.

I rolled my eyes and slapped her with the towel. "You're horrible."

"That's why I'm your favorite." Theia took a drink from the mason jar of Shine. "He may be a male, but if he keeps bringing good stuff like this, I just might learn to tolerate him."

I shook my head. "I'll talk to Bigfoot again tonight and see if we can hunt here again. I don't want to kill him, and I don't think he's being territorial."

Theia frowned. "You need to stop talking to the Swamp Ape."

"When Ella pissed him off is the only time he's even offered to cross the water. I seriously doubt I'm in any danger," I assured her.

"And I think the itch is making you delusional," she replied before taking another drink. "Do you think this would put Ella in a better mood?" She asked, wiggling the jar.

"Day drinking always puts Ella in a better mood." I was ignoring the comment about my itch. "We can go out there together; it may be safer for your face that way," I said as I opened the door.

As she walked by, she shot me a piercing glare. "Do you think he'd ask questions if we had him take us into the bayou again the day after tomorrow?" Theia asked as we rounded the house.

"Maybe. We can always tell him we want to fill our freezer while we can," I told her, wanting the coypu to ease my own itch.

"You really shouldn't let yourself suffer, not when there's an agreeable human around," she said before opening the barn door.

Ella abruptly halted her punching and fixed her eyes on us as we entered the barn. "What do you two want?" She demanded, addressing us for the first time since her fight with Theia last night.

"The human brought shine. It's called manipulation at its best," Theia offered, holding up the jar.

"Pimping out our sister for alcohol isn't what I would call manipulation at its best." Ella didn't move as she spoke to Theia, her voice tinged with anger.

"She didn't pimp me out," I said, crossing my arms. Ella had a way of making me feel dirty at times, and I didn't like it.

"Leave the jar and get out. I'm not ready to deal with either of you unless you're ready to fight." Ella's tone was dismissive as she turned back to the punching bag.

I sighed. "I figured." Theia sat the jar on the table, and we left Ella to her vice. "I'll go into town tomorrow and get Clay to take us out again if I can't get Bigfoot to let us go here without a fight," I told Theia as we walked back to the manor.

Theia and I spent the rest of the day doing things around the manor. When dark came, I made my way down to the dock. It was a little while before Bigfoot showed up. "Hey there, Big Fella, wanna hear about my day?" In response, he took up his usual position against the tree. "Well, Ella is pissed still. Clay, the boatman we hired, brought us some moonshine, which was good stuff. I had a good lunch with him. I was tempted to kiss him, but I didn't. It's complicated."

I stood there, nervously chewing my bottom lip as I weighed my next words. "It would be less complicated if I could just get a coypu and not have to see him anymore. I know there are some here, in this part of the bayou, if you'd let us hunt here again." He bared his teeth at me and shook his head in a firm denial. I let out a weary sigh, feeling the weight of our unspoken conversation between us.

"I'd ask why, but you can't really speak. I suppose we could play twenty questions. Is it because this is now your territory?" In response he gave another definitive shake of the head. "Is it because of something we don't know about out there, like the Grunch?" After a moment's hesitation, he nodded his head in affirmation. "Alright, will you let me know when it's safe to hunt here again?" Once again, he nodded, silently agreeing to my request.

"So, I guess, in a way, you are just trying to protect us," he nodded in agreement. "Thank you, but we have been taking care of ourselves for over twelve thousand years. We can handle it." I assured him. He bared his teeth at me, and I sighed. As I looked at him, I couldn't help but ask him again, "You still aren't letting us hunt here, are you?" Without any hesitation, he shook his head, 'no.' "I suppose that means I'll have to go into town in the morning and have Clay take us back out again," I muttered, gazing down at my lap. "I don't know how to face him after today." Just when I thought I had him all figured out, Bigfoot surprised me. He sat up and blew me a kiss, catching me completely off guard.

I let out an involuntary burst of laughter. "Did you just tell me to kiss him?" He shrugged and made a strange snorting sound, almost as if he were laughing too. "You and Theia are both ganging up on me. Dealing with this itch is hard enough, but with everyone pushing me to 'jump the damn boatman,' it's getting ridiculous.

"To be honest, if he didn't have as much restraint as he did, I'd probably have ended up with my tongue down his throat today." I confessed, feeling a rush of warmth on my cheeks. "The itch in my throat is craving much more than that. If I don't do something fast, I'm worried one of us will lose control." Leaning my head against the post, I thought of how Ella coped with her urges. "Well, Theia or I might lose control." Turning my head, I looked at Bigfoot. "Perhaps you and Theia are onto something; maybe I should kiss Clay. Maybe I can take the edge off the itch without going too far." I said thoughtfully as I gazed

up at the sky. "I think I'm going to call it a night now."

I grabbed the shotgun and returned to the manor without

looking back. I was certain Bigfoot would have vanished into the trees

if I had turned around to look. As I walked in through the kitchen door,

I shut off the outside light and walked into the living room, hanging the

gun on the way. Theia shot me the same judgmental look as last night

but didn't say anything. "I'm going to see Clay in the morning," I stated

before snagging the bottle of tequila from the coffee table and making

my way to my room. I disregarded the sounds of Theia's protests as I

shut my door and took a long swig of the bottle.

I walked into the bathroom, plugged the drain, turned on the

water, and undressed. It was a drinking-in-the-tub kind of night. As I

settled into the tub, I welcomed the sting of the scalding water on my

skin. Once the water was as deep as the tub allowed, I turned it off with

my foot and tipped the tequila back. This worm didn't stand a chance as

the thoughts of my past lovers filled my mind.

I'd lost lovers in nearly every century to violent deaths. The

Black Death had taken one; countless wars had taken others– wars

incited by Ares. A wild animal attack, hunting accidents, common colds, vendettas– all took a lover or two from me, but not a single one was taken by old age. I have never been brave enough to reach out to an immortal, either. Sitting the bottle on the floor, I sank under the water, trying to escape my tragic memories, only to find myself remembering my pirate lover whose ship had gone down in a storm with my sisters and me on board.

Raising my head from the water once more, I wasn't sure if my face was wet from the bath or tears. Tears of anger, pain, and fear. How was I supposed to pursue Clay knowing my past, with the bitter memories haunting me every time the itch began or a male caught my eye? How was I supposed to go into the swamp on his boat and not pursue him, knowing if I didn't, I may lose control and doom him to addicted servitude? A siren's call was a drug you couldn't quit. A siren's call would end a mortal's life if they didn't hear it every day for the rest of their life.

I took another long drink from the bottle and closed my eyes against the hopelessness of my existence. Soon, I would drive Theia into a bar to find a mortal to satisfy her itch. For whatever reason, mine seemed to be worse than hers. Ella lived with an itch. Every day of her life was a burning hell as she struggled to deny what we were meant to do.

Theia walked in then. "Don't take the tequila back; I need it tonight," I said to her as I held onto the bottle.

"You're starting to crack, aren't you?" She asked as she rolled up her pant legs, sat on the edge of the tub, and slipped her feet into my water.

Not bothering to hide it, I looked at Theia with all the distress and pain I felt. "On days like this, you and Ella are the only things keeping me alive."

"We all have days like that," she soothed as she took the bottle from me and got a drink herself. "I wasn't talking about your past haunting you, though; I was talking about the itch," she explained as she handed me back the bottle.

"Why is it so much worse for me," I asked, my voice tinged with frustration.

She rested her head against the wall and let out a sigh. "I'm not sure; I don't remember this ever happening. I know we forget things; if we didn't, we'd go insane with age." She raised her head from the wall and looked at me once more. "Don't get pissed at me for this, but do you think it's because of the boatman? Like, maybe you honestly want him, and it's making the itch that much worse?"

With a glare, I took a drink of the tequila and handed the bottle back to her. "I hate that you might be right. I hate that I keep doing this to myself. I hate what we are."

"I hate our mother and aunts for turning us out," she said as she took the bottle back from my hand. "I hate our father for manipulating us into starting wars and leaving us in Atlantis."

"Do you even remember what any of them looked like, other than Mom?" I asked.

She shook her head. "To be honest, I'm not even sure I remember her face correctly."

"Do you think Ella does?" I pondered, thinking about how she was lying in her bathtub right now, covered in blood from her self-inflicted wound.

"If she does, I think it's as a target. The hell we each went through in Atlantis wouldn't have happened had our mother not sent us away. The hell she went through made her bitter and filled with hatred for anyone but us. Sometimes, I even wonder if she might hate us."

As I sat there, drowning my sorrows in tequila, the weight of regret settled heavily upon me. "She hates that we didn't save her, I think." I murmured, my voice heavy with emotion. "That I didn't save her when I was so close to her all those years and didn't even know." Another swig of tequila burned its way down my throat as fresh tears welled up in my eyes, a bitter reminder of my perceived failure.

"You were under the Queen's constant watch. What could you have done? We were in a vulnerable position as three defenseless girls. Devoid of any supernatural abilities, immortal strength, or restorative powers, and lacking any combat training."

I asked gently, "Do you hate yourself too," I didn't bother wiping away my tears.

"Every day," she confessed. "I'm going back to gaming now. You should take care of your itch before something terrible happens for all of us."

Chapter 12

Kassie…

Morning came, and I left my hair loose, putting a little moose in it to help tame the frizz from the constant humidity in the early November air. Still in my pajamas, I went to the front porch where Theia and I sat in silence, while Ella was in the barn. After having my coffee, I returned to my room, got dressed, and looked at myself in the mirror. I hesitated for a moment before deciding to put on some makeup; I was stalling.

Closing my eyes, I told myself being nervous was stupid. We had tried running from the itch before but it hadn't worked. The only thing we could do was find someone to satisfy our physical desires. Clay was handsome, kind, and interested in me. We also needed to go back out to try to find a coypu. Even if the itch was taken care of for me, my sisters still felt it. With that thought in mind, I headed out of the manor and into town.

When I arrived at the docks in town, I turned off the ignition and just sat there, the itch roaring like molten lava in my throat. "Damn it!" I cursed under my breath as I slapped the steering wheel. Getting out of the truck, I stood straight and walked down the docks to find Clay. I had no idea what I was going to say to him, only that the longer I waited, the more I needed him, or anyone for that matter.

As I reached the end of the docks there were two males with Clay; one of them I remembered as Jack and the other was unfamiliar to me. Slowing my walk, I listened to what they were talking about.

"I already told you I'm on a retainer; I ain't taking nobody else along," Clay stated.

"You're on a retainer with three pretty little women, it's not like you can't take one more person on your boat; the divas will get over it," Jack insisted.

"I have no problem with beautiful women; I might even be able to teach them a thing or two," the stranger said.

Clay's face hardened. "Those 'divas' would hack you up into bait and toss you over the edge as we went through the bayou. Just because they are pretty doesn't mean they are easy to handle."

"Very well put," I said, walking up with a scowl on my face. The stranger snorted and I spun on him, "Part of the deal we've made with Mr. Higgons is that not even an animal is permitted on the boat with us. Would you want your contract violated?"

"I'm just wanting to hunt large gators; I'd think you ladies would appreciate an extra set of strong hands to pull in the day's kill."

"My sisters and I are stronger than we look." A smirk spread along my face, this pathetic mortal had no idea I could rip his throat out with my bare hands.

"A lot. The three of you were a little terrifying when you came back covered in blood from field dressing that boar," Clay said next to me. "They don't need any help, Sir; if they do, they have me. Jack can keep taking you out in search of that monster gator you want; I won't be doing it."

The two males scowled and walked away, their dissatisfaction evident in their body language. As they left, I turned to Clay and offered an awkward smile. "Thank you for that. I'm sorry if I've cost you a customer."

He tilted his head and frowned at me, "Why are you wearing makeup?"

I felt my face turning red as a blush crept across my cheeks. "I… well… does it look that bad?" I struggled to come up with a response.

"You look beautiful, wearing makeup or swamp muck," he said with a gentle smile. "Who's the lucky fella?" He asked, an edge to his voice.

Tilting my head, I gazed up at him. "Are you jealous?"

"I just want to feed the gators something nice, is all," he said with a smile, making me laugh.

"Do you wanna get something to eat?" I asked him.

A smile spread across his face. "I'd love to." We began walking up the docks toward the road again. As we reached the back of the main building, he suddenly grabbed my hand and tugged me to him. "Don't slap me for this," was all the warning he gave before his lips met with mine with a tender kiss. The itch roared to life in my throat igniting into a burning desire, and I couldn't resist clutching the front of his shirt and kissing him back. He broke the kiss and gazed down at me. "Damn, that was better than I'd imagined."

I found myself blushing once again. "I really am hungry," I admitted, pulling away from him only to have him snag my hand.

"I don't want to keep pretending we don't like each other. We can take things as slow as you want, but I'm done pretending you aren't the most stunning woman I've ever met."

I struggled to find the right words as fear and excitement coursed through me. "Clay," I found that I was at a loss for words and couldn't explain my hesitation.

"You've been hurt before, I get it; you don't have to explain. Just give us a chance."

Smiling, I nodded. Giving Clay a chance is the reasonI'd come to town, after all. If I used him to satisfy my urges, I'd feel guilty, especially after getting to know him. Feeling his hand wrapping around mine as we walked, I knew I was already in too deep to love 'em and leave 'em anyway. "How many jobs have you turned down since we contracted you?" I asked after a few minutes of walking.

"Two. This man, and one who smelled worse than swamp gas," he said with a smile.

"Oh wow," I laughed, amused by his colorful description.

"He said he was hunting the Skunk Ape and that the only way to find it was by the smell. Honestly, I wonder if the Skunk Ape wasn't just an unlucky Bigfoot who got gassed by something. Either way, the critter isn't doing any harm, so I don't let folks hunt those on my boat."

"So you believe in Bigfoot?" I asked, suddenly feeling a little awkward again. After all, Bigfoot was the one who told me to kiss Clay last night.

"The stories have to come from somewhere. I like to think a bunch of them are running around out there, untarnished by humanity," he told me as we arrived at a small diner.

"Good to see you speak so highly of the human race," I teased.

"You've met Jack," he teased back with a smile.

I laughed. "People like him are why my sisters and I don't socialize much."

Clay had led us to a cafe where we were seated by an older waitress. "I'll take my usual as soon as she's ready to order, Joane."

"Sure thing, Clay," she leaned in and said, "He's a real gentleman; don't find them like that no more," she said to me with a playful wink.

"I'll take whatever his usual is," I said with a smile.

"That's quite a spread hun; are you sure?" Joane asked.

"Two eggs benedict, biscuits, and gravy, topped with hashbrowns and bacon with a side of blueberry pancakes, to be exact," Clay told me.

"Why not, I'll take any leftovers to my sisters." I shrugged.

"Coming right up," Joane said as she smiled and walked away without bothering to write it down.

"Are you still trying to make up to Ella for me being there yesterday?" Clay asked.

"She will eventually get over it," I said.

"I hope so. I'd like to come over more often; and not to take you on dangerous boat rides," he added with a wink.

"Speaking of dangerous boat rides, do you think you could take us out again tomorrow? We want to fill our freezer while we can," I asked, nervously biting my lip.

"Sure thing. Do I need to come out and clean the gutters for Theia," he teased.

"I'm sure she would appreciate that, but she might get it done today," I said as Joane set a coffee pot,two cups on the table, and a dish of creamers. "Thank you," I told her with a smile.

"Why don't I head that way after we get done here? If she's already gotten it done by the time I get there, then you can find something else for me to do."

"Alright, do you want to ride out with me or take your boat?" I asked, nervously adding creamer to my coffee.

"I'll take my boat, I use it to get home. You can't get to my house with a car," he replied with a warm smile creasing his face. He seemed to be enjoying himself on our little date.

"Right." I responded as I mused over that thought before continuing, "Well, we always have yard work to do," I rambled, trying to make conversation.

"I'm sure. Why don't we talk about something other than business, though? Like, have you ever traveled before?"

"Oh, um," I hesitated before I answered his question. "My sisters and I traveled all over when we were younger," I told him, not technically lying.

"So, have you ever seen snow, like the deep snow you see in movies?" He asked.

I was grateful he didn't ask how old we were when we'd traveled or about our parents. "Does Alaska count?"

"Yikes! That sounds cold," he chuckled.

"It was, but the snow was beautiful," I assured him.

"I miss traveling. A few years back, I traveled through Virginia in the fall; it was amazing! All the colors! Don't get me wrong, Louisiana is great, but I like to experience all of it every now and then, you know?" He elaborated.

"Yeah. Maybe in a few years, my sisters and I will travel again," I said, feeling a twinge of guilt. Clay was mortal, which meant no matter how I felt about him, we could only be together for a short time. He deserved someone he could build a life with, not someone who would bring him constant danger and could never age with him.

"Why don't we talk about something else? I don't like that look." Clay's remark drew me out of my thoughts.

I smiled at him and nodded. "Sorry, not all of our travels have been good."

"It's a combination of the good and the bad that makes us who we are. I try to focus on the good memories or the here and now. Right now, I have a beautiful woman with melancholy written all over her face sitting across from me. Tell me about something that makes you happy, and if you can't think of something on the spot, then I'll tell you about my misfortunate frog gigging trip."

A genuine smile spread across my face. "Oh, this I gotta hear."

"Alass, I was just a youngster, not wearing any suspenders. In my cockiness, I'd decided that I would bring home a bunch of frog legs for my momma to cook up. The mud was deep and thick. As I went to retrieve the frog I'd nailed with my slingshot, the mud sucked me down nearly to my waist. I managed to grab a low-hanging tree branch and pull myself out, but I ended up walking home without my boots or pants, as they had been claimed by the swamp muck."

I couldn't hold back the laughter that erupted from me as Joane placed our plates before us. "That's golden!"

"Your turn to tell me a misfortunate hunting story and make it colorful," he said enthusiastically. We spent the rest of our meal discussing our various swamp adventures before he paid the tab and walked me back to my truck. "I'll see you at your manor. Might even beat you there," he said with a sideways grin.

"Probably, you don't have any traffic," I shot back with a smile of my own. He stepped closer to me and brushed a lock of hair behind my ear. "Are you going to kiss me again?" I asked.

"I was thinking about it," he confessed with a soft smile. "I don't want to push my luck though."

"Then how about a little pull?" I offered as I reached up and put my hand on the back of his neck, tugging him down for a kiss. His lips were soft against mine, his hands slipped onto my waist. I leaned forward into him and darted my tongue out against his lips. He groaned and thrust his tongue into my mouth. Instantly, I was wet, excitement coiling inside my core, the itch in my throat turning to a soft hum as my desires were beginning to be fed. *Fuck me, I want that tongue between my legs.*

He broke the kiss and cleared his throat. "This is going to be a lonely boat ride," he said with a smile. The itch in my throat roared back to life in complaint. I wanted nothing more than to fall into that kiss and all the physical pleasures it had promised.

"I'll see you at the manor," was my awkward response as he stepped away from me. Clay looked at me one last time before walking around the truck and starting down the docks. The morning sun cast his shadow in front of him on the wooden planks; his thick, muscled legs carrying his tall, broad frame further away from me. Giving myself a shake, I got into the truck and headed home, where I would meet up with him again.

By the time I reached the manor, I was a complete mess. The burning desire stirred by the kiss, the itch in my throat, and my nerves had me in a state of frustration. I'd even found myself rubbing my legs together at stop signs, the friction doing little to calm my heated body. I shut off the truck and got out, slamming the door harder than I needed to in my frustration. As I walked around the house, Ella walked out of the barn.

As she stood in the doorway of the barn, arms crossed and eyes narrowed, she questioned, "Did you fire the boatman after Theia tried pimping you out to him?"

I kept walking, not bothering to look at her, and replied, "Nope, I shoved my tongue down his throat and invited him over to clean the gutters."

"You did what?" She demanded behind me. When I didn't answer, I heard the barn door slam shut.

The sound of Clay's fan boat in the distance was the only thing that kept me from turning back to the barn to try and reason with her. Guilt twisted in my stomach over Ella's discomfort, but it was the price I had to pay for what I was and how I was. She would adjust to things in a few days, and I would be sure their interactions were limited, just as I always had. Never bring them home; that had always been my motto.

"Ooo, I hear a fan boat a'commin," Theia sang as she let the kitchen screen door smack shut behind her, the sound of the spring zinging in the air as the wood whapped and bounced on the frame. Every noise seemed to be amplified by my nerves.

"Yep, he said he'd clean the gutters," I informed her as I kept walking to the dock.

"You should give him a hand with it! Oh, and tell him to take his shirt off; it's hot work. That part's for you," she called after me as his boat appeared in the distance.

Without missing a step, I flipped her off. While neither of my sisters cared for men, they were polar opposites in how they handled my interests in them. Theia was supportive of finding release with a willing male, while Ella preferred bloodshed and constantly asked why I couldn't satisfy myself with females. Stopping on the dock, I leisurely leaned against the weathered post and watched with a smile as Clay pulled his boat up. "I thought you were going to be here before me, slowpoke."

"I had to deal with Jack before I could leave the docks in town; his jaw will be sore for a few days," he said with a smile.

I raised a brow curiously. "Care to tell me what happened?"

"He said some things I didn't like about you and your sisters, and I set him straight on the matter." After tying off his boat, he stepped onto the dock. "Those gutters aren't going to clean themselves," he changed the subject, obviously not willing to talk about it anymore.

"Theia was excited when she heard the boat; she even told me to help you. She hates cleaning the gutters," I elaborated, still feeling a bit awkward and horny as hell.

"She also really doesn't like men, even if she's decided I'm at least partially tolerable," Clay smiled good-naturedly.

"So, is this not awkward for you at all?" I prodded, wondering how he could be so calm.

"Hunny, it's been awkward from the moment I set my eyes on you; I'm just good at putting on a professional face," his smile again, but this time it dimpled on the right side of his cheek as he let his guard slip ever so slightly, and fuck did that smile make me wet.

"Wow, and here I thought Jack was the one I needed to worry about," I playfully teased, trying to make light of the fact that I was ready to ride him on the damn dock in broad daylight.

"Jack is a scumbag who isn't fit to fuck an old bar whore," Clay said bitterly, his good humor slipping into bitter disdain.

"I didn't mean to upset you; I was just teasing."

He let out a breath. "You didn't upset me; Jack did before I left the docks. I shouldn't have let that slip." He smiled at me, but it didn't quite reach his eyes this time. "Let's just get those gutters cleaned and talk about things we want to do one day, like climb Everest or explore the Aztec Ruins."

After that, Clay and I set to work cleaning the gutters. As the day wore on, we slowly made our way around the entire manor. By lunchtime, we'd managed to get three-quarters of the job done. Theia found us on the front side of the manor and sat two beers next to me with a playful wink. "Get you some, sis," she teased.

"Fuck off," I hissed at her with a glance at Clay on the roof.

"He can't hear us. Grab that cinder block, anchor the ladder, and climb up there with him. He ain't getting no younger."

"Just go away," I said with a roll of my eyes.

"Clay and Kassie, sitting in a tree, k-i-s-s-i-n-g," she sang as she skipped away.

Clay's hearty chuckle made me look up at him, mortified. "Your sister is just as horrible as mine." He remarked with a playful glint in his eyes

I felt my face flush with embarrassment. "How much did you hear?"

"I recognize the toon, is all. Was the rest better or worse?" He teased me.

"She brought us each a beer," I skirted the question.

He chuckled once more. "Grab one of those blocks I saw and bring them on up."

With a smile and shake of my head, I did as he and Theia had suggested. When I reached the roof and handed his beer to him, he smiled at me and patted the shingles next to him. "Yes, because I was so going to climb back down with my beer I just brought up."

Clay rolled his eyes and chuckled. "It was that, or start kissing you, but I feel like you may just toss me off the roof, if I keep pushing my luck."

"You have more wiggle room than that with me," I told him as I leaned in and kissed his bearded cheek.

"Oh no, the friend zone is painfully close with that one," he taunted.

"Shut up," I laughed. The two of us bantered with each other and drank our beers before I found myself leaning back on the hot shingles. Clay leaned in over me and kissed me. We were so engrossed that it wasn't until Theia came by singing that damn childish song again that we jerked apart.

Chapter 13

Kassie...

After Clay had finished the gutters and pulled a few wayward limbs from the roof, I walked him down to the dock. "I guess I'll see you tomorrow," he said as he shifted his weight from one foot to the other but didn't move to get on his fan boat.

"Bright and early," I replied, waiting for him to kiss me again. I was ignoring the itch in my throat that demanded I strip him of his clothing and satisfy my desires right there on the dock.

"Ah, hell," he muttered before crushing my body to his. One strong arm wrapped around my waist, while his other hand tangled in the back of my hair as he kissed me so thoroughly my toes tingled. I could feel the hard press of his erection against my lower stomach as our bodies pressed together in our embrace. Heat flooded between my legs, and my breasts ached as they pressed against his chest. My hands were fisted in his shirt as my mouth drank in his kiss, opening to the prodding of his tongue and tingling with excitement at the velvety thrusting over mine.

The loud slam of a door jolted us out of our embrace. Stepping back, quickly, I glanced back at the manor to see Ella storming over the lawn toward the barn, followed by a clearly pissed-off-looking Theia. "Fuck," I muttered. "I'll see you tomorrow, Clay; I need to go keep my sisters from killing each other."

"Yep. Night," Clay said as he stepped back, trying to discreetly adjust himself.

"Sorry," I apologized as I managed to pull myself away from the dock and head toward the barn, without watching Clay leave for once. I was just reaching the manor when I heard his fan start up, and I knew he'd be disappearing around the bend by the time I was in the barn.

"I didn't force her to do anything! You really think I would do that?" I heard Theia yell through the door.

"You'll want to back the fuck off before I turn you into my new punching bag," Ella hissed as I opened the door.

"Really, guys?" I demanded, feeling aggravated.

"Whatever," Theia snapped and shoved passed me, stomping back to the manor.

"Ella," I began in an apologetic voice.

"Just don't," she said in a deadly tone. With a sigh, I turned and headed back to the manor to try my luck with Theia.

"That stubborn, man-hating, selfish, cunt licking, *gah*," Theia seethed with anger as I entered the empty room.

"I fucked up, I shouldn't have invited him out here for anything," I said in an attempt to try to sooth the situation . It was important to me to at least calm one of them down.

Theia turned quickly to face me, her face contorted with her rage. "Don't apologize for one fucking day of him working and what, a little making out? It's not like you were fucking him in front of us! It's not like I held a knife to your throat and told you to go after the boatman, or I'd torture you!"

My sister had no idea what chord her words struck. "You and I both know how she is; she just needs a little time to cool off," I replied in a quiet tone

"Yeah, well fuck her. I'm feeling the itch, too, but you don't see me telling you to bring home a male for me! She knows you can't satisfy the itch with a female like we can, and neither of us are that into self-mutilation to take the damn edge off like she is."

"Theia, that's enough," I said sternly this time. "One pissed-off sister at a time, if you don't mind."

"Fuck you too; you don't get to tell me how to feel," Theia snapped before marching into the kitchen and blindly grabbing a bottle from the freezer.

Sighing, I turned away from my sister and headed into my room. Closing the door, I leaned against it and closed my eyes. If the persistence of my own throat was any indication, Theia and Ella were only going to get worse. Ella could manage her own curse as long as Theia and I didn't pick at the scab, but with Theia raging at her, it was only a matter of time before she would need to give in and find satisfaction with a willing female.

Despite my concern for my sisters, my body still ached with need. Knowing there was little I could do to soothe my sister's ire, I went into my bathroom, turned on the shower, stripped, and stepped under the hot spray. Closing my eyes, I imagined Clay kissing me, remembering the feel of his body pressed to mine, the tantalizing pressure of his erection through our clothing. Leaning against the shower wall for support, my left hand cupped my breast, and my right slid between my legs.

I imagined it was Clay's hand on my breast, his was probably rough with callouses and warm. Would he use his fingers between my legs like I was now? Remembering the press of his erection against my stomach, my breathing grew heavy and fast. I wanted to feel that erection thrusting in and out of me, hot and thick. I wanted it rough and fast with his large body over mine. I remembered the way his tongue felt in my mouth, the smell of butterscotch and bourbon that was his scent as I continued to strive for climax under the spray of the shower.

My release came with no little effort and did nothing to ease the empty ache inside. Shutting off the shower, I dried myself, and put on my pajamas. I grabbed my book and flopped onto my bed, reluctantly accepting that I'd be spending the rest of the day alone in my room, unable to satisfy my desires. This is just another downside of being a Siren.

***

In the morning, Ella was sitting on the front porch, and Theia was in the living room, anger hardening their expressions. Deciding I didn't want to deal with either of them, I dressed, grabbed a pop-tart, and took my coffee to the dock. I sat with my back against the post, where I would have sat the night before to talk to Bigfoot had I not locked myself in my room with my book. Part of me wondered if he'd waited for me last night, and I felt a pang of guilt.

Soon enough, the sound of Clay's fan boat drew me from my thoughts with a tingle of excitement. The itch had me feeling like a love-struck teen. Standing up, I smiled and waited as Clay pulled his boat up. "Good morning, beautiful," he greeted me with that half smile that was starting to make my knees weak.

"Well, it's morning, at least," I said, glancing back toward the manor.

"Your sisters are still fighting, I take it?"

"Yeah, they will get over it, but until then, there's just a lot of tension," I replied as he stepped off the boat and walked toward me.

"Let me distract you for a couple of minutes," he whispered softly, gently tugging me toward him with a mischievous glint in his eyes.

I couldn't help but smile and wrap my arms around his neck, feeling the warmth of his embrace. "You're going to make it hard for me to focus on the hunt today, you know that?" I teased, trying to keep a straight face.

"You made it impossible for me to sleep last night, so it's only fair," he said with a wink. No sooner had Clay begun kissing me, than my sisters were at the dock. "A quick kiss it is," Clay said before stepping away from me and back onto his boat. Theia and Ella, their expressions guarded, boarded the boat and deliberately tried to sit as far apart as possible, facing opposite directions. Clay gave me an apologetic look before starting the fan and steering us down the waterways into the bayou.

The fan hadn't completely shut off before Ella climbed out of the boat and headed into the marshy trees. Theia and I were left to catch up with her, the fan boat disappeared completely out of view before we closed the gap.

As we trudged through the swamp, I could feel the tension building in Ella. "When are you going to get off your fucking high horse and just get over it already," Theia demanded, unable to keep the silence any longer.

Ella turned and dropped her blade, throwing a fist at Theia's face. "Shut your fucking mouth."

"Ella!" I yelled at her in shock.

"Go get your clit sucked," Theia spat as she dropped the gun and charged Ella.

"You first, pimp!" Ella sneered.

"Man-hating-dike-cunt," Theia hissed as mud splattered and sticks snapped under the weight of their bodies as they hit the ground.

"Stop," I yelled at them as I rushed forward to break up the fight. Ella tossed her elbow back into my face before taking Theia to the ground. Staggering back a step, I held my nose and then pulled my hand away from my face and to see the blood. "Damn it, Ella!"

"Go fuck the boatman," Ella shot me a menacing look as she and Theia grappled, pulling eachother's hair and exchanging blows in the midst of the muddy chaos.

"She didn't do anything wrong," Theia shot back before forcefully sinking her teeth into Ella's tender arm.

"Bitch," Ella yelled and rolled Theia under her and began beating her in the face without restraint. I hurled myself at Ella, the two of us tumbled through the mud,splashing into the water. As I tried to stand up, I pulled moss from my face only to be met with Ella's fist. "Stay out of it," she yelled, as I splashed backward into the water.

I stumbled backward as I struggled back to my feet, rage tinting the edges of my vision black. Shoving my hair back from my face, I focused on my target Ella. Setting my jaw, I went to move forward only to have searing, crushing pain explode in my leg as I was dragged into the water. Swampwater filled my mouth and nostrils as my head slipped beneath the murky surface.

"Kassie," Theia and Ella's voices echoed as my head went underwater,filling my ears with the roaring sound of water. I twisted beneath the water and reached for the gator that had a hold of me, only to have another set of massive jaws clamp shut on my arm. Desperately, I struggled to get my head above water as the massive gators ripped at me, trying to drag me deeper. My head emerged above water in time to witness Ella attacking a gator while calling out for me.

My head sank beneath the murky water once again, with moss clinging to my face and free limbs, making it impossible to fight off the two gators. The gator latched onto my leg and then released with a sudden jerk as more tails, and massive gator bodies battered mine. I felt myself losing consciousness as water filled my lungs with a searing burn. The next thing I knew, the gator on my arm began to do the death roll. Suddenly, the gator's jaws were ripped apart, and my body yanked from the water. I had only a moment of relief before searing pain exploded with a cracking sound through my skull, and my world went dark.

Ella…

Guilt, horror, and rage roared inside me as I watched the gators snap and thrash in the water, our sister caught in their jaws. Theia and I struggled to reach Kassie as more gators snapped at us. Blood tinted the water where Kassie bobbed in and out of sight, two massive beasts fighting to rip her limb from limb. In my fit of anger, I'd recklessly led my sisters into the midst of a congregation of eight-foot immortal-eating reptiles.

"Kassie! Fight them!" Theia screamed as she too fought off the gators, blood and muck coating her as she rammed a stick into the eye socket of one.

"Kassie! I'm coming!" I yelled as I hacked at the one who sunk its teeth into my leg, too filled with adrenalin to feel the pain. Desperation filled me as I struggled to fight my way to Kassie. We could fight, but only if we could remain conscious. The gators had dragged her below the water, where she would soon black out and be at the mercy of the ravenous reptiles.

In all the commotion, Theia and I hadn't heard Bigfoot's crashing approach. The massive hairy creature shoved Theia backward before smashing a gator's skull with a single blow. His head swiveled toward me and then the other gators that were slowing my approach to Kassie. "Kassie! Save Kassie!" I raged. Without hesitation, he surged into the water. As I struggled to reach them, Bigfoot flung what must have been a ten-foot gator out of the water with a roar. His hands plunged beneath the surface again, and the top jaw of another gator went flying before my sister's bloody body was pulled from the jaws of what would have been her demise and draped over Sasquatch's shoulder. "Get her out of here!" I yelled at him, seeing her limp figure and feeling myself flooded with fear as still, more gators thrashed in the

water and on the bank.

Chapter 14

Kassie...

I woke to a searing pain shooting through my arm, and I instinctively jerked, my eyes focusing on Clay as he carefully peeled back the bandage encasing my arm. He looked down at me, his gaze full of concern. "Kassie, I was afraid you wouldn't wake up." A wave of relief washed over his features as he spoke, his expression softening.

As he rebandaged my arm, I took a groggy glance around the room and tried to make sense of my surroundings. The bedroom was inside a cabin, a single dresser set under a lone window, and the chair he was sitting in next to the bed was the only other furnishing. "How did I get here?" I asked, struggling to recall being pulled out from under the water, then a sharp pain as my head smacked off a tree.

"Bigfoot," he uttered softly as he settled on the edge of the bed and tenderly placed a kiss on my forehead.

When he pulled away, I blinked at him, and I noticed he wasn't wearing a shirt. His broad chest was lightly dusted with hair, and a line of the same dark curls led down into his low-slung pants. "Why aren't you wearing a shirt?" I asked dumbly, hating the persistence of the burning itch in my throat.

"Because I don't want to. You need your rest. Is there anything I can get you?" He didn't move away from me; he just sat next to me, looking at my lips like he was going to start kissing me again. I didn't want him to start kissing me again because I wouldn't want him to stop, the itch in my throat was more demanding than my pain, and I needed to get away from him before I healed in front of his eyes.

"You need to take me home to my sisters; I can rest there," I said, noting that my leg was also injured, but the pain wasn't as severe as my arm.

"No," he said, standing and pacing away from me. "You're not moving from that bed until you're completely healed," he insisted as he turned back to me. "You should be completely healed in a few days; it may take a little longer than that for your arm."

I blinked at him. "What are you talking about?" I asked, pretending to be clueless. Was he aware of my rapid healing? Had my injuries healed that much since they occurred so that he knew something was different about me? How long had I been unconscious?

He sucked in his bottom lip and looked out the window then down at the floor. "I know you're a Siren." He looked back up at me with no humor in his face.

"Did you hit your head or something? Sirens aren't real," I said, trying to act like a human would in this situation. How could he possibly know what I was?

He put his hands on his hips and looked at the floor momentarily as if trying to find the words to say, the sunlight coming in from the windows behind him. "And a Bigfoot didn't save your ass today." *Was he angry?*

"Clay, Bigfoot is nothing more than a myth. Nobody knows if he's real or not," I said, unsure what else to do or say.

"Myth? Myth!" He shouted as he shoved his pants down and stepped out of them. I began to panic, my eyes widening as he stepped back from the bed, completely naked. His body became hairy as he grew to nearly seven-foot-tall, his face changing into the one I'd thought I'd only ever see in the swamp. He was Bigfoot! Standing at the foot of the bed, breathing heavily, he stared down at me. He lunged forward, his hands landing on either side of me as I squeaked. He was shifting back over the top of me, looking me right in the eyes as he did. "I saved your life today; I will always save you!"

Before I could say anything, he was kissing me again, his naked body over top of me. The blankets and my clothes did little to stop the heat coming from his body, which was brushing against mine. My nose filled with the scent of butterscotch and bourbon, one that had my body tingling from head to toe, one that had me nearly shaking with need. "You're mine, Siren," he whispered in my ear as he gently kissed my neck. "How can I make you see that?"

I moved to shove him off of me and sucked in a sharp breath of pain as my arm failed to move. He was off of me in seconds. "Clay, I'm so sorry." He'd heard me singing, and now he couldn't let me go! I'd done what I'd sworn never to do again and entrapped a male!

He looked confused, his brow furrowing in concern. "You're the one who's hurt, not me."

I shook my head, feeling the guilt gnawing at me. "Not that. You heard me singing."

He looked shocked for a moment, then smiled and sat down on the bed next to me, still naked and *huge!* "I've heard all of you sing out hunting coypu that day. You didn't entrap me with your singing. You lured me with your scent," he said, closing his eyes and taking a deep breath through his nose. "It's intoxicating."

I blinked at him, feeling a sense of shock and disbelief. My smell? My smell! My eyes widened as I tried to process what he was saying. "You mean Bigfoots are like Werewolves? You scent your mate?" Inside, a part of me pleaded, *please say no, please say no!*

He smiled warmly and nodded, his eyes filling with admiration. "You are mine, and I couldn't be more pleased. You are the most captivating mate I could have ever hoped for."

"How can you be sure? I mean, maybe I just smell good or something?" I felt like I was spiraling. This mate business couldn't be true, and yet, my past still haunted me like a nagging ache, the reality that every male I'd ever cared for had died a terrible death.

His smile slowly faded as he gazed at me with intensity. "There is no mistake; you are mine. Am I not yours?"

"Sirens don't have mates. I'm only half Siren, but my dad doesn't have a mate either," I explained, feeling the weight of confusion and disbelief settling in.. The only true Sirens were those created by Posiden or born of Sirens and humans. He had to be wrong; I couldn't be his mate.

"What species is your dad? There are very few who don't have mates?" he questioned, his posture stiff as he stayed next to me, still *very* naked!

"Do you think you could put your pants back on? It's a little awkward," I covered my eyes. I was trying not to look at him, but heaven help me, I wanted to look at him. "What do you mean you've heard us all sing? I've never met a male who wasn't, um, entrapped."

"You talk to me while I'm naked all the time in my Sasquatch form," he said as he got up and pulled on his pants, leaving me with a mix of relief and disappointment as I peeked through my fingers. "Bigfoots don't have ears; we feel vibrations. Are you going to tell me who your dad is?"

"My dad is one of a kind. I'm sure you've heard of Ares," I said, feeling a little better now that he had pants on. It wasn't much, but clothes were clothes. He heard... in vibrations?

"Ares, as in the God of War?" He asked, his eyes widening in astonishment. I nodded silently, confirming. "That means that you and your sisters are the only ones of your kind unless he has bred with other Sirens," he concluded, his voice tinged with curiosity and intrigue.

"No, just our mother. Her name is Teles. She is one of the ten sirens brought to life by Poseidon, not Achelous," I told him. Since humans could find this information, I didn't feel wrong telling him.

"Then you have no idea if your kind have mates or not. You are mine, so you must have mates," he told me as he circled the bed and lay beside me, his arms folded behind his head. "That also explains why you and your sisters are as battleworthy as you are."

I attempted to move away from him but failed; I was still in a great deal of pain, my arm not fully reattached, and my leg must have been worse than I realized. "What are you doing?"

As the sun dipped below the horizon, casting long shadows across the landscape, he turned to me with a weary expression. "It's getting dark outside. I was going to relax a little before getting us some dinner. I've been too worried about you to even sit since saving you from those gators." His voice carried a hint of anger as he spoke those last words.

"I'm not staying here," I informed him.

He sat up, his piercing gaze locking with mine as he responded, "You're not leaving," he tone laced with stubborn determination; that edge of anger I'd heard becoming more prominent in his command for me to stay.

The stubbornness was so unlike Clay that I was thrown off for a moment. "Clay, I need to get back to my sisters." I pleaded, hoping he would understand the urgency of my situation.

"You're not leaving this cabin until you are completely healed." He said firmly before continuing, "Your sisters know that you are safe. They watched me save you and kill the gators. Hell, Ella even told me to get you out of there!"

"My sisters! They were fighting the gators too!" I exclaimed, suddenly filled with panic as images of the monstrous-sized reptiles attacking my unarmed sisters flashed in my mind. Pain seared through me as I struggled to sit up in the bed.

Clay gently pushed me back down. "They are fine. I made sure of it before getting you out of there. I wouldn't have left your sisters to perish."

As I gazed up at him, I felt the need to surrender to the pain and allowed myself to lay back down. "Thank you," I managed to say.

"Just rest. You are all safe for now, and your sisters will need to heal as well, although neither of them was injured nearly as badly as you," he assured me, the edge of anger coming back as he pointed out my injury. *Was he mad at me for getting hurt?*

"Clay, I need to get back to them. We haven't been separated in twelve thousand years," I said, my voice tinged with urgency and a hint of desperation.

"Did you just say twelve THOUSAND years?" He asked incredulously, turning onto his side and looking at me with raised brows, his eyes widening in disbelief.

"Give or take," I admitted sheepishly, feeling a flush of embarrassment creeping up my cheeks. I'd never discussed my age with anyone.

"That's a long time to go without a night away from each other. My sister and I would have killed one another," he smiled at me. "I haven't even lived near my sister for a few decades now. My family moved away to more secluded parts when this area became more populated. They also spend most of their time in Sasquatch form."

"We fight a lot," I admitted with a sigh. "It's worse than normal right now." I felt heat rising to my cheeks as I felt myself blush.

"Because of the itch? That's what you called it, right? It's not always easy to translate the vibrations correctly."

I closed my eyes. "I regret talking to you now."

He chuckled softly, his eyes sparkling with amusement. "Don't say that. Our talks at night have been the highlight of my existence."

Opening my eyes, I turned my head and glared at him. "You tricked me. I thought you were some sort of immortal animal, not a shifter with the ability to transform, and sure as hell, not my boyfriend."

"Mate," he gently corrected with a warm smile.

"Sirens don't have mates," I retorted.

"You do. I also did my best to communicate with you in that form. I was a little afraid you'd turn me away if you knew too soon. I mean, you and your sisters aren't exactly fond of males," he said pointedly.

"When we lose control, males are in danger. We can't lift the entrapment, it's until death and can even cause death. Why wouldn't we keep males at a distance?" I explained, hating myself all over again for what I was.

"I feel like there is more to it than that. Ella hates males, while you and Theia seem to not trust us," he looked at me, his eyes softened.

"You can trust me, Kassie. I'll never do anything to hurt you. I'm also not easy to kill."

"Thank you," I said with a weak smile. He'd just made a promise he couldn't keep. The Fates would take him from me somehow, too.

"You should rest now. I'll get us some dinner soon. I just had to know you would be alright," he readjusted so that he was facing the ceiling and closed his eyes. We stayed like that for about fifteen minutes before Clay sat up and brushed his hand over my hair. "I'm going to go cook us some dinner now. If you need me, I'll be just outside the door in the kitchen."

"Clay, um, I may need your help getting to the bathroom. I think my leg can support me, but I don't think I can sit up on my own," I admitted, feeling embarrassed.

"Your leg is pretty bad; it may not support you at all until morning," he told me as he quickly got out of bed and helped me into a sitting position. "I'll be your crutch to the bathroom. You should be able to use the counter for support once you're in there, so you can have some privacy."

"Thanks," I gritted out through my pain as he helped me stand, wrapping his arm around my waist and guiding me out of the bedroom door. I glanced down and noticed that he'd carefully cut away most of my pant leg to tend to my wound. We made our way slowly through the small kitchen with its tiny table pushed up against a wall and a wood-burning stove on the wall next to the bathroom door. Clearly, he lived alone and didn't spend much time in his cabin.

He got me inside the bathroom, and I braced myself on the sink. "You got it?" He asked, his voice laced with concern.

"Yeah, I've been through worse," I reassured him with a smile.

His face hardened. "Don't tell me that; I still want to go back and shred every gator in the swamp."

"So you're mad at the gators?"

"I'm angry that I wasn't closer and that you got hurt at all. I should have been there the whole time. Go to the bathroom; I'll put some water on for spaghetti."

"Oooh! Do you have meatballs?" I asked excitedly.

"I sure do," he told me with a nod, accepting the subject change as he stepped out of the dimly lit bathroom and closed the door behind him.

Once the door was latched, I let my guard drop, feeling the weight of exhaustion and pain settle over me. Pain radiated throughout my body like a relentless storm. Not only were my wounds burning with every movement, but my muscles and lungs ached, a reminder of the swamp water that had filled my mouth and lungs. Carefully pushing my pants down, I sat on the toilet with no little effort and looked at my leg. Clay had bandaged my lower thigh and calf and cleaned up the blood and grime that must have covered my skin. Bruises covered most of my legs, and when I lifted my shirt, I noted that my abdomen was covered in bruising as well, along with some pink marks showing my skin had been broken.

The memory of the gator's bodies banging into me as their jaws clamped down on my limbs seeped into my mind. Had Clay not saved me, I very well would have died, leaving my sisters to eternity without me. The state of my clothing was deplorable. Stiff and encrusted with dried blood and swamp muck, they seemed to weigh me down even further. With a heavy sigh, I attempted to wipe away the filth before struggling to gain my feet. The sheer effort it took to pull my pants up was not just embarrassing but also a stark reminder of my physical state. My unbuckled belt hung loosely as I limped over to the sink, which offered a brief respite as I washed my hands, my injured arm utterly useless in the process.

Clay's voice carried through the door. "Are you alright in there? Do you need me?"

"Fuck off, Clay, I'm not a damn child!" I snapped, feeling irritable because of my pain. I closed my eyes, realizing I had snapped at him for no reason. "Sorry, I don't deal well with healing."

"Can I open the door now?" He asked, not responding to my outburst.

"Yeah," I sighed, feeling the weight of exhaustion as I leaned against the counter. My gaze fell upon the sorry sight of my ruined clothing, splattered with blood stains and mud that wreaked of the swamp.

Clay gently turned the doorknob and entered the room, and leaned on the door frame. He eyed me empathetically, "Healing is a bitch, I get it. I think my sister left some clothes here the last time she stayed. They will be big on you, but they are better than what you're wearing."

"Are you calling your sister fat?" I teased, putting my mask of humor back in place.

He responded with a knowing smile. "No, she's quite a bit taller than you."

"Must be a Sasquatch thing," I joked.

He chuckled and said, "No, you're just really short."

"Fuck you. I take back my apology from earlier."

He chuckled. "How about after we eat, I run you a bath so you can wash the rest of the grime off?"

"That would be nice," I admitted as he helped me to the kitchen table.

"Are you alright here, or do you want to be propped up in the bed?" He asked.

"Clay, I swear to the Gods, if you don't stop fussing like a mother hen, I'll kick your ass with my good arm," I said with a glare. He held up his hands in surrender. "Thank you," I turned and looked out the window that the table was pushed up against, taking in the darkening swamp as he cooked. I could feel his eyes on me as I gazed out the window into the darkness. How much had I told him in his Bigfoot form? Had he told me the truth from the start would I have pushed him away? Would I have opened up to him in his human form? I couldn't shake off the worry about what my sisters would think. Would Ella go as far as to kill him?

Clay placed a plate in front of me. "What are you thinking about, beautiful?"

"Your death," I admitted with a blank expression.

He raised a brow. "Do you intend to kill me?"

"No, but Ella might when she finds out the truth. I'm pissed at you for not telling me, but I also understand why you didn't." I looked down at the plate in front of me. "Would you have told me had I not been injured today?"" I asked, hoping for an honest response.

"I was trying to figure out how." He replied, as he sat in the chair across from me.

Shrugging, I swirled the spaghetti on my fork trying to ease the tension. "You could have always told me when we were drinking on the roof, or in the diner, or even this morning before I got on your boat."

"Kassie, I wanted to tell you, I wanted to tell you from the moment I saw you, but you are the first person outside of my family to know. We don't go around exposing what we are to anyone. Not immortals or humans. You should understand that better than anyone."

As I nodded my head, I looked up at him with a mix of curiosity and apprehension. "I guess you have a good point there. Now that we both know the truth, do you promise not to keep secrets from me?" Why was his answer so important? Was I still going to pursue a relationship with him? I'd never had a relationship with an immortal. The thought was both thrilling and terrifying at the same time.

"As long as they are my secrets to share. I don't expect you to tell me your sisters' secrets," he replied, locking eyes with me.

"That's fair enough," I responded, feeling a sense of relief at his understanding.

"As soon as you're done eating, we'll figure out how to give you a bath," he smiled weakly at me. "I'll only help when you ask for it, no matter how painful it is for me to watch."

"You learn quickly," I said around a mouthful.

"I imagine a shower might be easier for you to get in and out of without me, but all I have is the clawfoot tub in there." We fell silent for a few minutes as we ate before he broke the silence again. "You should be able to turn the water on and off with your good foot, so you should maybe get in first and then start the water. When you're ready to get out, I'll help you so you don't slip."

"I'll figure out how to get out of the bath on my own, thank you," I said, feeling my face turn red.

"If you slip, you risk ripping your wounds open," he said sternly.

Turning to look out the window again, I gritted my teeth against the fact that he was right before turning back to him. "So help me, if you sneak a peek at anything, I'll carve your eyes out of your head."

<u>Chapter 15</u>

Kassie…

 After dinner, Clay and I managed to get me in and out of the bath without reopening my wounds. To my surprise, Clay had not tried to catch a glimpse of me that I'd noticed. However, the itch in my throat nearly choked me when he'd helped me out of the tub. I'd drained the water and wrapped myself in the towel before calling for him to help. His strong arms wrapped around my nearly naked body, pressing me to his exposed chest as he'd lifted me from the tub, almost pushing my restraint over the edge despite my injuries.

 He left me to get dressed on my own, looking as flustered as I felt as he'd closed the door. Cursing my useless arm, I struggled to pull on the pants. Surprisingly, they were only a little big around the waist, a small victory in the midst of my frustration. Next, I carefully pulled on the shirt, wincing through the pain of maneuvering it over my injured arm first. The real agony came when I tried to pull the shirt on the rest of the way, the fabric tugging on my injured arm and sending sharp pain radiating through my arm, chest, back, and neck. I sat there for a few moments, relief washing over me as I welcomed the temporary escape from the pain, even if it only offered a brief distraction from the persistent itch.

"Kassie? Are you alright?" Clay called through the door. His voice was muffled by the wood, but I could still hear the concern in his tone.

"Yeah," I called back, trying to sound steady.

"Can I come in?" Clay's voice was softer this time, filled with a gentle concern.

"Sure." I looked down at myself, feeling small and vulnerable in the too-long pants and too-big shirt. I hated how pathetic I must have looked. Clay entered the room and wordlessly knelt in front of me. "What are you doing?" I demanded.

"Rolling the pant legs up so you don't trip. Just shut up and let me help you a little," he said, trying to be helpful despite my resistance.

"I don't like you right now," I retorted, giving him a stern look.

Unfazed, he explained, "I'm not going to apologize for taking care of you in just a few small ways. It goes against everything in me to allow you to struggle in any way, so be thankful I haven't been smothering you," as he continued to carefully roll up one of my pant legs.

Narrowing my eyes, I reached out and flicked him on the forehead with my good hand. "Prick."

He looked up at me in shock and exclaimed, "What the hell, Kassandra?"

I let out an exasperated sigh and tilted my head back, gazing up at the ceiling. "Sorry. My sisters and I tend to pick fights when we are frustrated." Sexually and painfully frustrated, but he didn't need to know that.

He leaned in, forcing me to meet his gaze. "I can smell your particular frustration, and it's driving me mad."

My face flushed crimson, and I snapped, I couldn't contain my emotions any longer, "Fuck you."

"At your pleasure, beautiful, but you are not in the physical state if I'm not mistaken." My lips parted in shock as I looked down at him, a rush of heat flooding through my body and the itch in my throat screaming at his words. He sat back and looked up at me, his eyes darkened. "Kassie, being this close to you is driving me mad. The animal in me doesn't care that you're injured or that you haven't given consent; it only cares about the scent of your desire."

I swallowed hard as I held his gaze, "Clay, right now the itch in my throat doesn't care either. It doesn't even care who you are, so long as you can sate my desires. This itch," I gestured to my throat, "it's so much worse than just an itch. It's more tormenting than the pain of my injuries. Every breath I take may come back out as the Sirens Call, entrapping any male who hears it for the rest of their existence. Not even my death would release the victims."

"Then why do you deny your desires?" He asked after a moment of silence.

I glanced down at my lap, feeling the weight of the words I was about to share. "Every male I've lain with has died a terrible death." I confessed. The memories of loss and pain flooded my mind, but I knew honesty was necessary. I met Clay's concerned gaze as I continued, "It's not something I take lightly." The confession constricted my chest, but Clay deserved the truth. The weight of my past experiences lingered in the air as I revealed my deepest fears to him.

"Bigfoots aren't easily killed. I'm over four hundred years old, if that helps," he assured me with a soft smile.

"And you believe I'm your mate. What happens if I have no feelings left for you after I've been satisfied? Will you be able to let me go?"

Clay exhaled deeply. "It was too late for that the moment I caught your scent. I can never move on but I can keep my distance and watch over you. I can be there for you the next time you feel the itch." Clay maintained unbroken eye contact as he spoke.

The itch in my throat was more demanding than ever, and after a moment's hesitation, I inquired, "Do you understand that I can't promise you anything more than tonight?"

He raised his brows, "Tonight? Kassie, your injuries are too extensive for that. Why don't you get some rest, and we can talk about this in the morning?"

"Alright," I agreed, closing my eyes and nodding.

"Let me help you to bed," Clay said softly. He wrapped his strong arms around me, supporting my tired body as he lifted me easily to my feet. Despite the pain, we shuffled awkwardly and silently out of the dimly lit bathroom and into the softly lit bedroom.

"Clay, I hate what I am, hate that I can't tell you what I truly feel," I admitted.

He wordlessly helped me into the bed before brushing his knuckles over my cheek. "I don't hate what you are because it's enabled you to live long enough for me to find you. You will eventually be able to discern your true feelings for me, and should they place me into the 'friend zone,' I will happily live that life as long as I can be near you. But that's a discussion for another day."

"Clay, where are you going to sleep?" I asked as he straightened.

"I was going to sleep on the couch. I don't know that either of us can be trusted to sleep in the same bed right now," he said with a half smile before walking out of the room, his footsteps echoing into the small living space. I closed my eyes and leaned my head back on the pillow. Clay had no idea how complicated my life was. I couldn't be his mate because I couldn't leave my sisters. For different reasons, the three of us only lived for each other.

My chest grew tight as the thoughts swirled in my head. Clay was kind, patient, and handsome. In all my centuries, I'd never even been able to remain friends with a male without them suffering a terrible fate. I didn't want that for Clay or myself. I couldn't tell him the

truth, couldn't tell him that the itch had little to do with how I felt about

him. The itch didn't cause me to enjoy talking to him;that came

naturally. I enjoyed everything about Clay except the impending doom

his association with me would bring him.

Chapter 16

Kassie…

I'd fallen asleep with guilt and lust tightening my chest. The guilt triggered dreams of my life with my sisters. For millennia, the three of us had relied on each other, living for one another, and searching for Ares. After what happened to each of us in Atlantis, we'd all been left shattered, using each other as our only reason to keep going, the only part of our existence that wasn't torture.

The aroma of food roused me from my dreams and memories. The bedroom door was ajar, and I could hear Clay moving around in the kitchen. Without thinking about what I was doing, I attempted to sit up, only to gasp at the pain in my arm. I let out a growl of frustration and slumped back on the pillows as Clay rushed through the door.

"What happened? Are you alright?"

"Just need to bash some gator skulls in," I said bitterly. Why the hell did it take so long for things to knit back together, but a broken neck was just a couple of hours of healing?

Clay rolled his eyes and said, "Breakfast will be done soon, and I have coffee too."

"What do you think I was getting out of bed for?" I asked with a wry smile, feeling a twinge of amusement despite the discomfort.

"You're still healing. Let me help you to the table," Clay said, his concern evident in his voice as he reached out to assist me. I glared at him, unmoving.

"My leg is almost back to normal; my arm will need a few more days. I can walk just fine." I insisted, trying to reassure him as I struggled to sit up without putting weight on my bad arm. Clay, seeing my determination, held up his hands in defeat and stepped back from the bed. "Thank you," I said, appreciating his concern even as I swung my legs over the side of the bed. "See, ye of little faith," I added with a hint of playfulness, knowing that his worry stemmed from genuine care.

"I've never seen anyone heal that quickly," he said as he stared at my leg as though he could see through the pants to inspect my wounds.

"I guess that's just the only perk of being a daughter of Ares," I said with a nonchalant shrug, followed by a wince as pain radiated through my arm that was still reattaching itself.

"I see your arm still needs a little more time to heal, though," he observed with a frown, his brows furrowing with concern. I had a feeling that no matter how stoic I tried to appear, he would notice my reactions to every hint of pain. "I give it four days tops," I replied, determined not to show weakness, even though the pain would last for long after the visible wound had healed.

"Is that how long it will take you to stop limping?" He asked with narrowed eyes as I started to walk into the kitchen.

"End of the day," I shot back bitterly. That was the deadline on how long I would give myself to cover up the limp.

He sighed and rubbed his face with his hands. "You don't always have to be strong, you know. I won't fault you for healing."

"Only the strong survive. I've had twelve thousand years to learn just how true that is," I told him as I walked into the kitchen and glanced around for a coffee cup.

The early morning sunlight filtered through the windows, casting a warm glow over the kitchen. Clay walked over and opened a cabinet by the sink. He pulled out two blue and white speckled mugs, the kind that looked like they had seen many mornings like this one. "I have some milk in the fridge, no creamer, and I have a little sugar in that dish there," he said as he pointed to a little wooden croc with a lid behind the coffee pot.

"Just milk for me, thanks." I said as I poured the coffee with my uninjured hand and then reached for the milk in the fridge. Despite Clay's disapproving presence by the sink, I was determined to make my coffee on my own. Clay stood by the sink with his jaw locked as I got the milk and shut the door with my elbow. Setting the milk down on the counter, I struggled to open the top with just one hand and poured some into my coffee. As the ivory-colored milk swirled into the black liquid, I watched as it slowly transformed the deep hue into a comforting shade reminiscent of warm, sandy earth, creating a soothing swirl in my cup.

"You can leave the milk out for me," Clay said before I could put the cap back on. I narrowed my eyes at him but made my way to the table with my coffee, cursing under my breath as it sloshed over the rim and onto the wooden floor. Behind me, I could hear Clay pouring himself a cup of coffee. I turned to look at him, half-expecting him to add milk to his coffee, although I knew from our solitary date at the diner that he preferred it black. He tossed a kitchen towel over my spilled coffee before returning his attention to the milk. To my surprise, he whisked it into a bowl to make scrambled eggs.

"Were you planning on making scrambled eggs, or did you decide to do it so I wouldn't have to put up the milk?" I asked pointedly.

"I have bacon in the oven along with biscuits. Scrambled eggs topped with cheese are just a normal way to round out the meal," he explained without looking at me, his focus was on scrambling the eggs in the pan.

Frowning, I asked, "Why do you have the bacon in the oven?"

"In case you needed me, when you put it in the oven, you don't have to watch it, just wait about twenty minutes, and it's done," he admitted, a hint of concern in his voice as he tried to make things easier for me.

Closing my eyes, I felt a wave of mixed emotions flood over me. I was overwhelmed with gratitude and a tinge of shame. Clay had risked his safety and saved me from the gators, cleaned and dressed my wounds without taking advantage of me. Despite everything, he was doing everything in his power to keep me comfortable. He'd reassured me that my sisters had safely escaped the gators. Despite my less-than-pleasant demeanor, he continued to put up with my bad attitude. "I'm sorry I'm being difficult," I murmured, feeling a pang of remorse for not being more appreciative of his unwavering support.

"You're in pain and used to having to fight to survive. I've spent a lot of my life alone, with just the visits with my family members here and there. I understand," he said softly, turning his attention from the stove to look at me.

"Clay, I'm afraid, all the time. I'm afraid of losing my sisters again, afraid of falling in love with someone and destroying what I have with my sisters only to lose the male who came between us," I confessed in a quiet voice, my words heavy with emotion. This was a truth I had yet to share with my sisters. I felt compelled to reveal it now, driven by a mixture of guilt and respect. An admission I was unable to keep to myself for some reason.

"Kassie, I wouldn't do anything to come between you and your sisters, you know that, right?" Clay assured me, sincerity in his eyes.

"You don't understand because you are a male. Ella can't even stand you being on our property," I told him, feeling like my heart was breaking. I'd only known him for a handful of weeks, and yet I felt like I was growing dangerously close to him in ways I hadn't done with another in centuries.

"She doesn't seem to mind when I'm in my Sasquatch form. Not to mention, I think she may warm up to me once she figures out the truth," he said as he plated the eggs.

"Or she'll kill you for lying to us," I muttered. Ella was always looking for a reason for bloodshed. The fact that she'd not tried to kill him during our initial encounter that first day in the swamp was astonishing to me.

"She can try, but I'll just let her tire herself out, and when she's ready to talk, I'll explain myself as best I can." He pulled the bacon and biscuits out of the oven then and finished plating everything. "We have eternity for her to warm up to me," he added as he sat the plate down in front of me.

"Clay, she's hated males for as long as I can remember," I confided, gazing up at him with a tinge of sadness in my eyes. Despite his unwavering optimism, I felt compelled to be realistic. No matter how I felt about him, we couldn't be anything more than a fling, and even that was dangerous.

He gently pressed his lips against my forehead. "She doesn't know me yet. I don't know what happened to the three of you; I don't need to know because I will spend the rest of my existence protecting you." He searched my face for a moment. "That also extends to your sisters because they are what you love, and I'll always protect what you love." With that, he stood and walked to his seat. "Theia, on the other hand, is the one I'm really worried about killing me when she finds out the truth."

"Theia?" I asked in surprise.

"She hates me in my Sasquatch form and only tolerates me in my human form for you. At least Ella likes half my personality; well, what qualifies for liking someone in Ella's eyes," he said with a half smile. I rolled my eyes and just restrained a small laugh from escaping. "It's true. She wants my furry pelt as a throw in front of the couch."

I burst out laughing, unable to contain my amusement. "Oh, my Gods! That's the most absurd thing I've ever heard!"

His nonchalant shrug in response indicated that he didn't find my reaction surprising. "It made you laugh, didn't it? Also, it's kinda true. Then again, they may join forces against me when they find out the truth, then I'm in trouble."

"What about me?" I inquired with a quizzical expression, raising one eyebrow in curiosity.

His piercing gaze met mine as he leaned back in his chair, a sly smirk playing on his lips. "I'd let you beat me into submission any day," he replied, his voice laced with a hint of mischief. With a casual grace, he lifted his cup of coffee to his lips, taking a leisurely sip as he held my gaze, the air crackling with unspoken tension.

I narrowed my eyes at him, ignoring the roaring in my throat. "Once I get some food in me I may just beat you with the plate for that one."

He chuckled. "And here I was thinking we could sit outside and have some more coffee after we ate."

I grinned, feeling a tinge of playfulness. "I admit that your plan sounds better than mine only because my dominant arm is still healing,"

"In the interests of saving my floor, however, I am going to insist on carrying your coffee out for you," he said absentmindedly, his attention shifting between his food and our conversation.

I gave him a look before I glanced down at his scuffed-up floors. They had obvious wear, and he'd already cleaned up the coffee. "Enjoy your loopholes while you can. I'll be fully healed in no time."

"How long do you and your sisters plan to stay in this area? I'll need to be moving on sooner rather than later as well. Having to move every few years makes life interesting but lonely. Can't make any real connections with humans, especially when everyone is out to catch a Bigfoot," he added with a smile.

"How about when humans and immortals alike fear and hate you?" I asked without looking at him, unable to fully mask the bitterness.

"Other immortals don't know much about my kind either. As far as I'm aware, I'm the first of my kind to have a mate who isn't either human or Sasquatch."

"Why do you keep hidden from other immortals?" I asked, needing to know why his kind had alienated themselves.

He shrugged and said, "We just have as far back as I can remember. My mother told me that power and the constant fight for dominance consumed other immortals. We are a simpler race. You'd be hard-pressed to find a Sasquatch who wasn't basically a happy hippy who only resorted to violence when necessary."

"A happy hippy?" I repeated, trying to understand Clay's description of himself but failing.

He smiled at me, his eyes lighting up with enthusiasm. "We are kind of like tree spirits in a way, connected to these swamps. The areas in which we are born are the areas in which we are strongest. The further we get from them, the weaker we become until we are as weak as normal immortals. That makes us very aware of the environment and respecting nature."

"And here I was picturing you smoking a bong, hugging a tree, and singing Kumbaya."

He started to laugh. "Not exactly, but I do get a little worked up when people dump waste and garbage into the swamps."

"In my defense, those Grunch heads and critter bits are biodegradable."

He shook his head and grinned. "I hope you know I was only trying to show you that I'd taken care of all of them."

"I appreciated the gift. I froze one of the heads and then used it to take out my frustrations with an ice pick," I admitted coolly.

"That explains the smell," he said with a smile, arching a playful eyebrow.

Without hesitation, I picked up a biscuit and threw it at him. He stared at me, momentarily shocked, before throwing it back at me. "Hey, I made those from scratch!"

I pursed my lips. "Most females don't take kindly to being told they stink."

His eyes darkened as he looked across the table at me. "You smell like a blend of hibiscus, vanilla, and with a hint of lemon. I'd hardly say you stink."

His unexpected admission caught me off guard, leaving me feeling slightly exposed, a blush threatening to burn my cheeks. "What do my sisters smell like?" I inquired, my curiosity piqued by his confession.

"Hibiscus and rage. Their scent is less defined for me because they aren't my mate. I can also smell the rage in your scent, but it's not as strong. When I kiss you, the taste of vanilla and lemon linger on my lips." Heat flooded my body, the itch in my throat threatening to choke me.

"You smell like butterscotch and bourbon," I murmured softly as I looked up at him from under my lashes. "And you taste like butterscotch when I kiss you."

His eyes darkened intensely as he looked across the table at me. "Good to know."

Licking my lips, I pushed back my plate and stood. "Clay, if I don't find an outlet soon, I'm going to lose control of my powers and call every male within earshot."

His jaw tightened as he regarded me. "Kassie, you're still healing."

Rolling my eyes in disgust, I began limping forward. "You have a choice: you can either be gentle, or I can hobble into the swamp singing Crazy Bitch by Buck Cherry and see what happens."

He shoved his chair back so forcefully it toppled over. "Damn it, Kassie," he muttered, pulling me into his arms and crushing his lips against mine. I could feel the raw desire radiating from him, yet he was careful not to touch my injured arm. His fingers tangled in the hair at the nape of my neck. With his other arm wrapped firmly around my waist, he pulled me closer, his hips pressed against mine as his tongue explored my mouth.

As I slipped my good arm between us, I attempted to undo his pants but a frustrated growl escaped against his lips. He released my neck and slid both hands down to cup my ass before effortlessly lifting me. Instinctively, I wrapped my legs around his hips and draped my good arm around his neck while awkwardly keeping my injured arm bent at the elbow and pressed against his shoulder. As he carried me towards his bed, Clay dragged his lips away from mine and began planting soft kisses down my neck. Tilting my head back, I welcomed his nipping kisses to my throat and collarbone.

He gently laid me down on the bed, continuing to kiss my neck as his hands began to roam my body. The itch grew more intense every second I was near him, touching and tasting him. I couldn't resist any longer; I reached out and slipped my hand beneath his shirt and raked my nails across his back. "Lose the clothes," I rasped breathlessly as I arched my back, needing to feel his skin pressed against mine.

Without hesitation, Clay rose and stripped off his shirt, revealing his chiseled chest and abdomen. In a swift motion, he pushed down his pants. Then, he leaned forward, his fingers finding their way to the waistband of my pants, his darkened eyes locking with mine in a silent request for permission. I responded by lifting my hips, and he skillfully pulled my pants down, letting them fall to the ground. His lips grazed the tender red skin where my wound was almost healed. "Liar, I can still see the mark," he remarked, before his hands traveled up my shirt, and his lips danced over my stomach.

"It's just a scratch," I breathed, shivering at the exhilarating caress of his lips against my sensitive skin. My core throbbed as a wave of desire surged within me as his warm, rough hands glided up my sides, and helped me out of my shirt. The sharp pain in my shoulder quickly faded and was replaced by a delicious pleasure of his teeth lightly tugging on my nipple. His hands explored my body as his mouth moved from one breast over to the other. In response, I traced the contours of his form with my uninjured arm, eager to explore every inch of him.

"I want to taste every inch of you," Clay's voice was thick in my ear as he leaned forward on one arm and slid his hand down my body, his fingers slipping inside my aching core. A moan escaped my lips as I arched into his hand. Without thought, my good hand slipped down his body, my fingers wrapping around his thick erection. His breath caught in my ear, his voice low and filled with yearning. "Gods. Kassie, you drive me mad," he breathed each thrust of his fingers deepening my pleasure,, his teeth and lips tormenting my neck, collarbone, and ear.

Pleasure rippled throughout my body as I felt myself nearing release when suddenly his fingers left me. Clay's gaze locked onto mine as he slowly sucked his fingers clean, an act that left me breathless. I licked my lips, feeling impossibly turned on. The sight of him savoring my essence stirred something primal within me. "I was right; you taste as good as you smell, like vanilla and lemons," he said, his voice low and tantalizing. As he readjusted himself, the head of his throbbing erection brushed against my body, teasing against my aching core,igniting the fire of desire deep within me. I released my stroking hold on his member and slid my hand up to his shoulder, arching my hips in unashamed need. I craved more.

With a deliberate and painfully slow motion, Clay slipped inside, a groan escaping him as he settled as deeply as possible. My core stretched to welcome him, a moan of pleasure escaping my lips as he filled me. As he began to move, the rhythm of his hips, his teeth nipped at my neck, and his hand found its way to gently knead my breast. I reciprocated by nibbling at his chest and collarbone, lifting my hips to meet his every thrust. Tension and pleasure coiled within me, building like a tightly wound spring, and just as I thought I might burst, he slipped his hand between us, teasing that delicate sensitive little nub.

"Clay," I gasped, a wave of pleasure crashing over me as I felt myself teetering on the edge of release. Waves of ecstasy surged through my body, intense and shuddering, yet he continued the motion.

"That's it, Kassie, cum for me, love," he breathed against my neck. His relentless movements persisted, his devilish fingers tormenting me into a second, explosive climax. As the waves of my orgasm began to subside, he repositioned himself, lifting me to wrap my legs around his waist, his cock buried in me. His hands firmly gripped my hips tightly as he began thrusting faster and harder. Just as I felt myself shatter apart into a third orgasm, Clay thrust as deep as he could and held me tight as his hips jerked against mine in his release.

Through the hazy vision caused by the three explosive orgasms, I looked up at Clay. His eyes were closed, his head tilted toward the ceiling, and his breathing was as heavy as my own as we struggled to catch our breath. At that moment, his earlier words echoed in my mind,—"*cum for me, love.*" Love, that word, that dangerous, heavy word, was a knife in my chest.

Clay looked down at me then, the soft smile that had started to curve his lips fading as concern etched his features. "Did I hurt you?"

Chapter 17

Kassie…

"Not yet," I whispered, looking up at his still frame. He peered down at me, puzzlement etched on his face as he gradually disentangled our bodies. "I could use another bath. Would you care to join me?" I asked before he could question what I'd meant. He didn't need to know that mere mention of that one tiny word had sparked a deeper fear within me more than the terrifying experience of being dragged underwater by gators. He had no idea that each time that word had been uttered by a male, they had perished within days or even hours later.

Clay closed his eyes and chuckled. "Kassie, I don't mind getting a bath with you, but I don't think your body is quite ready for round two."

Smiling, I pushed aside my fear. "I was just thinking that you needed to get cleaned up as well; I think things got a little... sweaty." I mused.

A self-satisfied grin spread across his face as he said, "That they did." However, his expression quickly shifted to one of worry when he noticed my arm. "Kassie, I need to check your wound," he said, moving as I reached for my bandage.

"Shit," I muttered as I glanced at the now pink bandage. Our sex had numbed my pain but had reopened my arm. The bandage that was once pristine white now bore the evidence of fresh blood seeping through. "I didn't even realize it had opened back up," I confessed.

He frowned deeper at my words as he carefully unwrapped the bandage. "We should have waited a few more days."

"Well, this has been fun. Once I get cleaned up, you can take me home," I told him, not liking his response. I was a big girl. I could make my own damned decisions.

He looked at me with narrowed eyes before shifting his gaze back at my arm. "It doesn't look too bad. I think maybe it was just the friction rubbing it open. It's incredible that it's already scabbing over like this." He remarked, expressing genuine surprise.

"Clay, you better be taking me home," I said in a warning tone.

"I will take you home when your arm looks like your leg and you have full motion back," he said as he got off the bed and grabbed the bandaging I'd failed to notice on the dresser.

"I'm not a damn child! You don't get to make decisions for me!" I snapped.

He sighed. "Kassie, you said that it would only take about four days, won't you stay with me for just four days?"

"Clay-" I started to argue, but he cut me off.

"Three more nights," he interjected firmly, "just to ease my mind."

Looking out the window, I thought about what he was asking as he rewrapped my arm. Would three more nights be so bad? No, but that was the problem, wasn't it? I closed my eyes and berated myself for lacking the strength to distance myself from the pain he would inevitably cause. "Fine, I'll stay, but my sisters are not going to be happy with either of us."

"They can kick my ass from one end of Louisiana to the other if it means you'll stay until your arm is healed more," he said as he secured the bandage.

I laughed in response. "They will take you up on that offer. Ella thrives on a good fight."

"I noticed she was in the barn with the punching bag when I came over to help with the gutters." He noted.

"Theia loves playing war games on the Xbox. I'm the least violent of the three of us. That doesn't mean I don't know how to fight," I added quickly.

"I wouldn't expect anything less from the daughter of Ares, God of War," he said with a playful smile lighting up his features as if bearing such a title were a badge of honor. "Now, what about that bath? We're both still naked."

"Really? I hadn't noticed," retorted, my voice dripping with sarcasm as I crossed my arms, exaggerating my indifference. The cool air contrasted sharply with the heat radiating from my skin, a reminder of our earlier antics. Deep down, I wrestled with my feelings about my father, feeling a wave of resentment bubble up, but I chose to keep that part of my history buried from him.

Clay shook his head, his brow furrowing with concern. If he were anyone else, I'd be worried he'd start forming wrinkles with all the worrying and fussing he was doing over me. "I'll go start the water and be right back."

I rolled my eyes, the irritation bubbling just beneath the surface. "I think I can make it to the bathroom on my own, Clay," I replied, taking a steadying breath. Even though my body ached, I refused to show any weakness.

He held up his hands in defeat, his expression softening. "I was just trying to help. I've spent most of my time with injured humans, not immortals."

"What about your kind? You can't tell me you've never been injured before." I narrowed my eyes, challenging him to recall a time when he had been vulnerable. After all, we all had our battles, regardless of our nature.

"My kind don't have to be strong in front of each other. We are a tribal race. When one of us gets injured, the rest of the tribe takes care of them until they are healed, so that they can heal faster. The more you strain your injuries, the harder it is for them to heal," he said before walking out of the room, the weight of his words lingering in the air.

I supposed it was his way of telling me I was being too stubborn. As I rose to my feet, I walked slowly and deliberately toward the bathroom, feeling the tension in my muscles with each step. I'd made it only halfway by the time Clay walked back in the room. "You are a tribal race. I'm not," I told him, wanting him to understand the point I was trying to make.

"You're wrong. You and your sisters are a tribe of your own," he said, a hint of a smile playing at the corners of his lips. He stepped closer, his presence warm and reassuring as he matched my pace, careful not to interfere. I winced slightly with each step, managing a determined limp toward the bathroom, the tile floor cool beneath my feet. I could sense his concern, yet he respected my independence, holding back the instinct to offer a steadying hand. The bond we shared was palpable—complex, unspoken, yet unyielding. All the things I was trying *not* to feel.

"We didn't always have each other," I admitted, my voice trembling slightly as I reflected on our darkest days. Twelve thousand years had passed since those times in Atlantis, yet the memories still haunted us, resurfacing with every quiet moment triggered by our trauma. I swallowed hard, preparing for a recollection that seemed more complicated than masking my limp.

"We were separated for ten long years in Atlantis, each having no one but ourselves to navigate a world that had suddenly turned cold and unforgiving. I was luckier than either of my sisters; I was forced to serve the Queen of Atlantis, living in the opulent palace filled with shimmering jewels and rich tapestries. Yet, even in luxury, I was not free from torment." I paused, taking a shaky breath as I continued my retelling.

"When I failed to fulfill my duties, I was punished. The whip was a cruel but common tool of discipline, its biting sting a merciless reminder of my position. It never struck hard enough to leave scars, the Queen valued her beautiful servants too much to mar their flawless skin. Still, the pain lingered, a constant reminder of my servitude and the fragility of my existence. Each lash a grim reminder of my isolation, while my sisters battled their own demons somewhere in the depths of Atlantis." At this point, I was staring off into space while my memories silently tormented me. I was fighting back the wave of emotions that threatened to rush to the surface.

"Kassie," he choked out, too many emotions in his voice to decipher. "As long as I live, I'll never let anything like that happen to you again."

We were silent as he helped me into the tub. I didn't protest at his assistance; my mind was too consumed with thoughts of my past. He climbed in behind me, and I leaned against his chest. As I closed my eyes, I fought against the tears that threatened to spill. Clay was warmth and comfort, while I was death and torment to him. "You can't love me," I said as I lay there in his arms, the warm water soothing my aching muscles.

"And why is that?" He asked his voice gentle as he pressed a damp rag against my damp hair, the gentleness soothing my troubled thoughts.

"I'm not worth your love," I replied softly, my heart heavy with doubt. "I'll stay with you these next few days; we can have a short fling, but then we should go our separate ways."

He stopped wetting my hair with a rag before I felt his lips press to the side of my temple. "Then I have three more nights to convince you otherwise," he murmured, determination thick in his voice, as the weight of his words hung in the air between us.

My eyes burned with the urge to cry, and I shook my head. "I'm cursed, Clay. Everyone who has ever loved me has died. I was forced to watch my first love die inside an iron bull. Throughout my existence, I've watched too many males die for me. I refuse to watch you die."

He was silent for a moment and I braced myself for him to voice his unwanted sympathy. "How many males have been immortal? How many have claimed you to be their mate?"

With a heavy sigh, I lifted myself from his chest. "It doesn't matter," I said softly, "I've told you why this can't be more than a few days of sex. When I'm better, I'll return to my sisters, and we will leave the swamps."

A low growl emanated from his chest, catching me by surprise. "This will never be *just* sex between us, and I'll follow you to the ends of the Earth, waiting for you to realize that I'm not as weak as the rest of your *lovers*." He bit out the word lovers like it was bitter on his tongue before continuing, "I'll wait an eternity for you to realize that I'm the only one worthy of *your* love." I couldn't contain my emotions; tears began to stream down my face at his heartfelt declaration, and I quickly covered my face. Unlike the other males who had witnessed my rare tears, Clay didn't try to soothe me with empty words or question my sorrow. Instead, he enveloped me in his arms, pulling me close to his chest. "Just let it out. I'm here."

Chapter 18

Kassie…

Clay had let me cry before we'd finished the bath. I'd allowed him to help me out without complaint. Now, we found ourselves on his porch, the early morning sun casting gentle rays through the trees, creating a soothing atmosphere.

We sat side by side in comfortable silence, sipping on steaming mugs of coffee. I wore one of Clay's shirts, the fabric soft and slightly oversized, wrapping me in a sense of security.. The lingering scent of the bath combined with the rich aroma of coffee filled the air, wrapping us in a cocoon of warmth and quiet companionship.

"How many places have you traveled?" Clay asked, his curiosity breaking the silence.

I couldn't help but laugh at his question. "Clay, the real question should be, where haven't I been? At first, it wasn't easy to get around; we had to stay in one or two countries because of the language barrier and the difficulty of navigating unfamiliar cultures."

"Alright, how about, where are some of your favorite places you've lived?" he countered.

I leaned back on the porch swing next to him, contemplating his question as I pursed my lips. "That's a tough one. I've enjoyed my time here, but I like the colors of fall leaves. Maybe Kentucky, most recently. While I miss the food, I never want to see Greece or Rome again as long as I live. The place we had in the English countryside about two centuries ago is one I also miss."

"What happened to that home?" He asked.

"Neighbors started to notice we hadn't aged. That is almost always what happens," I said as I stared into the swamp.

"I've rarely been out of the swamps. Like I told you before, my power comes from them. It takes a while, usually months, for that power to diminish. However, we can draw energy from trees that grow in swampy areas."

"I don't think anything dampens our powers other than having our vocal cords cut," I told him honestly. "And a weakness toward water critters."

"If anyone ever tried to do that to you, I'd destroy them," he said quietly.

"My sisters and I have taken care of each other this long," I replied with a sad smile.

"Now I'm here to aid with that. I'm a tribal creature, remember?" He added with a reassuring smile.

Sighing, I looked out at the swamp again. "I care about you, Clay; I can't keep telling you how temporary this is between us."

"You can say that all you want, but I'm not going anywhere. You can run as far from the swamps as you want. I can become weak like an average immortal, but I'll stay by your side."

"You'll die, Clay; they all do," I said as I got up from the swing and limped to stand on the edge of the porch, leaning against the beam.

"I'm hard to kill, in case you haven't noticed," he remarked playfully from behind me, his hand sliding warmly onto my hip, anchoring me in the moment.

"Let's talk about something else," I suggested, giving him a faint smile that didn't quite reach my eyes. "Tell me about your adventures; how old are you? What is something you want to do that you haven't?"

He let out a low chuckle, the sound rich and deep. "I'm around four hundred years old, and there is a lot I haven't done actually. My kind doesn't get out much, as you are aware."

"Do you have to shift?" I asked, recalling how Werewolves were unable to deny the compulsion to transform on the full moon, while urges simply drew to Lycans but could deny it to an extent.

"No, I don't have to, I miss it though. That form is a part of me, makes me feel free, I guess."

"Then you could travel as a human and have your own adventures. No one would ever need to know you're even immortal. Not that humans know about us anyway, but other immortals wouldn't need to know."

"I wouldn't want to do it alone." He stepped closer to me, pressing himself against my back. His lips brushed my ear. "You could show me your favorite places, and I could scratch your itch for all eternity." A surge of excitement coursed through me, igniting a warmth deep within. My arousal flooded my body, heating and pulsing in my core. "Once you're fully healed, that is."

"If I were healed, I'd have you right here, right now," I said, pushing back the twinge of pain at his impossible suggestion. The longer I was with him, the more danger he was in.

Without warning, he scooped me up in his arms effortlessly, causing me to squeak in surprise. "Allow me to take the edge off for you," he said with a mischievous grin playing on his lips as he moved toward the door. Clay carried me through the kitchen and into the bedroom before laying me down on the bed. It dawned on me that he could scent my desire, stirring an intoxicating mix of excitement and embarrassment within me. He climbed onto the bed and positioned himself above me, his gaze locked onto mine. "You can stop being afraid of losing me. I'm not going anywhere."

I offered him a teasing, suggestive smile and said, "Here I was thinking you were going down."

His eyes darkened as he gave a soft chuckle, "You've got me there." Clay's lips pressed to mine as one of his hands slid between my legs. My hips instinctively arched towards him as I tangled my fingers of my good hand in his hair, feeling the warmth of his body against mine. As his fingers slipped into my folds, a moan escaped my lips even as his tongue slipped inside my mouth and danced with mine. One finger, then another, slipped inside me and curled, hitting that sweet spot inside as the heel of his hand worked his magic on my clit. Waves of pleasure washed over me, the tension in my core building as he expertly matched the rhythm of his fingers with the passionate movements of his tongue.

His lips pulled away from mine, trailing soft, teasing kisses down my throat while his free hand lifted up his shirt I was wearing, gently kneading my breast. As he shifted his position over me slightly, his mouth found my other breast, sucking my nipple almost to the point of pain before he playfully nipped at the tip and flicked his tongue over it. I gasped, then moaned, trying to arch my body into his touch despite the limitations with my damned arm. "Gods, Kassie, those sounds are driving me fucking crazy," he murmured, as he kissed and nipped his way down my torso, his light beard tickling against my sensitive skin.

He withdrew his fingers from my core and looked me in the eyes as he sucked them clean. "You taste so damn good," he said before gently settling himself between my legs. I could feel the warmth of his breath against my skin as he rubbed my clit with his thumb. When his tongue glided along my slit, he shifted his thumb aside and enveloped my clit with his mouth, teasing it softly with his teeth. His name left my lips on a gasp, as I fisted the sheets tightly, and my hips rising off the bed in response. His thumb returned to my clit, rubbing in slow, steady circles while his tongue dove in and out of my pulsing core. With his other hand, he lifted my ass slightly, allowing him to reach deeper. The combination of his thrusting and flicking of his tongue, coupled with the rhythmic caress of his thumb over my clit, quickly built the pressure within me. Before long, I found myself overwhelmed with pleasure, releasing on his tongue. He growled against my core, relishing every drop as he licked up my juices.

As my body ceased its rhythmic movements against his mouth and the tension in my core relaxed, Clay planted a kiss on my thigh. "Best breakfast a male could ask for," he remarked playfully.

Laughter escaped my lips between pants as I tried to catch my breath. "Shut up." I replied, a smile tugging at my lips.

"Sorry, did you want something else for breakfast?" He asked, grinning at me, as he laid comfortably between my legs.

"Maybe a nap at this point," I replied, my tone laced with amusement, a satisfied smile on my lips.

"Have I worn you out then?" He shot back, a playful gleam in his eyes.

"Yes, you are entirely exhausting to deal with," I teased in a haughty tone.

He let out a light laugh as he propped himself up onto his elbows. "How about I grab a book, and we can lie here and read it?"

I arched an eyebrow at him and teased, "Are you going to read me a bedtime story?"

With a playful glint in his eye, he replied, "I thought you might read to me since you're older," He had the audacity to wink at me.

Rolling my eyes, with a scoff, I playfully smacked his shoulder. "You should never comment on a woman's age!"

He let out a soft laugh. "I'll be right back." As Clay placed a gentle kiss on my thigh, he slipped out of the bed and left the room. A few minutes later, he returned with a copy of *The Hobbit* in hand. "Nothing like a classic," he said, grinning as he settled back down beside me. I frowned and shot him a skeptical look. "You know I'm not going to read it to you, right?"

He chuckled again, and I realized I could listen to that laugh for a lifetime. "I'm going to read it to you, you are the one with a healing arm after all."`

"Really? I'd forgotten," I said, my voice dripping with sarcasm.

"Just as I'd thought, I'll have to remind you for the next couple of days so that you don't hurt yourself all over again," he remarked playfully.

"Fuck you, I'm not that weak," I retorted defensively, feeling my irritation bubble up.

He held up his hands. "Easy there, I didn't mean it like that."

I squeezed my eyes shut and took a deep breath to steady myself. "Sure. What about that book?" I finally replied, trying to rein in my irritation. I was trying hard to make an effort to stop being a bitch.

"Kassie, you know I would never call you weak," he assured me gently.

"I think you mean, in a hole in the ground, there lived a hobbit," I retorted with a hint of bitterness.

Clay let out a small sigh. "It's like you've read this book before," he said, a warm smile spreading across his face. Why was it so difficult not to get attached to him?

"It's a classic," I countered, echoing his earlier sentiments, relieved that he was moving on rather than provoking an argument or fight like my sisters often did.. Clay then settled onto the bed, wrapping his arms around me. Resting my head on his chest, I closed my eyes as he began to read, letting the vibration of his voice lull me to sleep. The process of healing was utterly exhausting.

***

In the days that followed my recovery, Clay and I found ourselves forging a deeper connection. We shared stories about our adventures, reading, and indulged in a significant amount sex, lots of mindblowing sex. While the wounds on my body faded and disappeared, a weight settled in my heart. I knew I needed to distance myself from Clay to protect him, but each attempt to create that space was met with his unwavering determination to stay by my side. He made it clear that he would not be easily dismissed and that there was essentially no getting rid of him.

As sunlight poured through the window, I found myself nestled against Clay's chest, savoring the warmth and comfort of the moment. It had been four days, meaning today was the day I went home, and my agreement with him was fulfilled. "You know, we haven't finished the book yet?" Clay's voice interrupted my thoughts, catching me off guard as I assumed he was still asleep.

"I didn't know you were awake."

"You could stay one more day, so we can finish the book. I can take you home in the morning," he suggested, his fingers gently weaving through my hair while his eyes remained shut.

"Clay," I said weakly, a sense of anxiety washing over me. I wasn't quite sure how to respond. The truth was, having him near put him at risk. Wherever I went, whoever I encountered was always in danger, and involving him felt unfair. Everyone was always in danger when I was around.

"Kassie, you can run as far and as fast as you like, but I'll follow you. I'll keep my distance if that's what you want, but I'll be there, watching over you and your sisters."

A tear slipped down my cheek just as his eyes opened. "Clay, you can't. I told you, I'm cursed." I murmured, struggling to contain my emotions. The lump in my throat was painfully obvious.

"And I told you I don't care," he said, sitting up. I gazed up at him, another tear escaping down my face. "Kassie, I refuse to live without you. Getting to know you over the last few weeks only made that clear to me." He gently brushed away the tear on my cheek. "If you need time, I understand, but I'll be close by."

"I can't lose you," I said in a pained voice.

He gave me a soft smile. "I'm immortal, love. You won't lose me so easily."

I looked at him, uncertainty lingering in my voice as I asked, "First thing in the morning, you'll take me back to my sisters?"

"First thing in the morning," he promised. "Now, let's make something to eat!"

Smiling, I shook my head. "Do you know me so little? I need coffee before I do anything else."

He chuckled. "I thought we could drink the coffee while we cook. It will take a while for the biscuits to bake anyway." Clay swung his legs off the bed, and made his way to the dresser, the metal handles clinking as he rummaged through a drawer for a pair of pants. I watched as he pulled on the jeans, not bothering to put on boxers. It made sense for a shifter like him; boxers were just another item to take off or change. After closing the drawer, he opened another one, grabbed a shirt, and tossed it in my direction. "When you're done eyeballing me, put a shirt on," he teased before shutting the drawer.

With a smile on my face, I pulled the shirt over my head. "You like the way I look at you," I told him as I pushed my arms through the sleeves of his t-shirt.

"Correction, I love everything about you, including the way you look at me," he replied, making his way back to the bed, bracing himself with a hand on the wall, and planted a gentle kiss on my forehead.

I rolled my eyes in mock annoyance as I got out of the bed, playfully nudging him away. "You're such a girl."

He raised an eyebrow, his hands finding their way on my hips as I stood there. "Oh really?"

"Yes, now get in the kitchen and cook my breakfast, woman," I joked, enjoying the playful banter.

A mischievous spark flickered in his eyes as he grinned at me. "I think I've spoiled you in just four days." Before I could react, he lifted me off my feet by my waist, causing me to squeal in delight. "With a smile like that, I might just have to allow you to make fun of me," he remarked, carrying me into the kitchen and placing me on the counter next to the coffee pot.

"We should have had that thing set up to brew on its own." I remarked, giving the empty pot a mock glare as if it had personally wronged me.

"I've been a bit distracted, what with tasting vanilla and lemon every night," he replied, playfully pinching my thigh as a cheeky grin spread across his face.

A startled gasp escaped my lips as I swatted his hand away. "Stop that, I want coffee first."

"First?" Clay cocked a brow at me while he pulled down the filters and can of coffee from the cabinet.

Smiling, I nodded. "Yes, coffee first, then breakfast."

"Are you offering to feed a different appetite?" He asked in a suggestive tone, while his eyes darkened with lust as he glanced between me and the coffee he was preparing.

"If you're a good little housewife," I teased, giving him a cheeky eyebrow wiggle that made him chuckle.

"What about actual food? We burnt off a lot of calories last night," he countered, still grinning.

"Oh my Gods, you are a woman! You're turning down sex!" I feigned shock.

"Not exactly, I was wondering how you would taste covered in jam or honey. Maybe both," he said, struggling to suppress a smile.

"Sounds like breakfast is going to get sticky," I remarked in a soft, breathy tone, feeling my heart race and warmth wash over me. How was it that in four days Clay had started to bring to life the fantasies I'd envisioned with him for weeks? He filled the coffee maker with water and hit start before positioning himself between my legs. His hands slipped beneath the minimal fabric of my shirt, gripping my hips firmly. As he leaned in to kiss me, my fingers tangled into his hair. He began kissing me, and I surrendered to the moment.

Normally, my lust would subside once the itch in my throat was relieved, but for the last four days, my lust had been insatiable. The itch wasn't there, but the burning need deep in my core remained. I was Clay's mate, but was it possible he was mine as well? In the years we'd lived on that island with our mother and aunts, there had only been victims of the Siren's Call. As Clay's lips traced my throat, my head tilted back, and I found myself wondering if perhaps, just maybe, he *was* mine. He truly belonged to me. Or he was simply exceptional at bringing me to ecstasy with giving me earth shattering orgasms.

Epilog

Kassie...

    As the dawn of a new day broke, I found myself facing a crucial decision. Though long ago I had been enamored with Noaki, I struggled to recall feeling the intensity I'd experienced before. The thought of separating from Clay made me almost sick to my stomach with dread. My memories of Naoki were filled with sweet, exciting moments, while my connection with Clay could only be characterized by a deep longing and comforting warmth. With Clay, I felt a sense of completeness that both thrilled and terrified me. As I climbed out of the bed I slipped on the shirt I'd only worn briefly yesterday. I could sense Clay's gaze on me, but he wasn't saying anything. The air was thick and heavy between us as he watched me in silence.

I'd made my decision. It was a decision that Ella and Theia weren't going to be pleased with. I decided I was going to try to make things work with Clay. Truthfully, I didn't have a choice. Clay had made it abundantly clear that he would follow me to the ends of the earth; I was his mate.

"Want some coffee before I take you back to your sisters?" He asked, finally shattering the quiet tension that lingered between us.

Glancing over at him, I grinned and said, "I'll make it while you get dressed and find me some pants. Also, did my shoes make it?" I'd not worn shoes since waking up from the attack. The boots I'd been wearing when we'd gone hunting had been new, too.

"No, but I can take you home in my Sasquatch form so you don't have to walk. You'll have to carry my clothes though, unless you want me to be naked in front of your sisters."

"Right, it shouldn't be too hard to hold onto some pants and stuff," I said as I left the room to make coffee. I was such a coward! I couldn't bring myself to tell Clay what my decision was, because I was still haunted by my past and terrified of him being killed somehow. A sigh of frustration left my lips as I pulled the coffee down from the cabinet. *Fucking grow a set!* I thought to myself.

"Kassie, you don't have to have coffee with me if you don't want to," Clay said as he peered out of the bedroom at me, misinterpreting the cause of my sigh.

"I love you and you can't fucking die on me," the words spilled out before I could think, but I wouldn't take them back. I didn't regret saying it.

I took a deep breath and met Clay's gaze, determination in my own, "I want this to work. I want you to stay a part of my life. The thought of losing you fills me with dread, but I know you won't leave me. So, I'm going to cherish every single moment we share. And when you take me home, I'll tell my sisters about us."

He emerged from the bedroom, still naked, and enveloped me into his arms. "I love you, Kassie," he declared, and before I could fully process his words, his lips were on mine. The intensity of his kiss sent my head spinning as he held me tightly, raising me onto my tiptoes to deepen the kiss. I wrapped my arms around his neck, responding eagerly despite the dull ache in my arm and kissed him back. With a surge of exhilaration, I leapt up, my legs encircling his waist as he supported me. To my surprise, he didn't carry me to the bedroom, but instead, laid me back on the kitchen table. As he pushed my shirt up, one of his large, warm hands found my right breast while his other lifted my hips just enough for him to slide his erection into me.

My back arched as a moan escaped my lips. "You're mine, Kassie," he said as he pulled back and thrust into me. "Tell me you're mine," he demanded in a tight voice, his thumb rubbing my clit.

"I'm yours," I managed to breathe out, lost in the moment. The table shook with each powerful thrust as he continued to drive into me, his thumb skillfully circling my clit while his other hand caressed my breast. "Clay, yes!" I gasped.

"Kassie," he groaned, out burying himself deeper inside me, his hand shifting from my clit to grip my hip. His movements became more urgent, each thrust sending waves of pleasure through me until he finally reached his peak. At that moment, my body responded in kind, a powerful orgasm taking hold of me as well. As I lay there on the table panting, I opened my eyes to find him with his head thrown back, his chest rising and falling as he worked to catch his breath.

I reached my hand up to grasp the wrist of the hand that rested on my breast still. His eyes opened and he looked down at me. "You're mine, Clay," I said, laying claim to him, something I had never dared to do before.

With a grin on his face, he leaned forward and pressed his lips to mine, then effortlessly lifted me up from the table and carried me to the bathroom. "I'm yours," he finally said as he sat me on my feet.

I couldn't hide the smile on my face as I asked, "What about the coffee?"

He returned my smile, planting a quick kiss on my lips before responding,"You start a bath and I'll start the coffee," With that, he stepped out of the bathroom, leaving me with a comforting ease in my heart.

We enjoyed a warm bath together, making love again in the bath, then had coffee on the porch before I got ready for the day. Clay handed me a bag heavy with his clothes, then shifted into Bigfoot form. "Well, hello there Big Fella, care to give me a lift?" I teased with a playful grin. He let out an amused snort before scooping me up in his arms and setting off into the swamp. It took us nearly two hours before we reached my home. After navigating the water near the dock, Clay gently set me down on my feet. I took a deep breath, gathering my composure as I started to walk toward the house, feeling the soft moss of the lawn beneath my bare feet.

I turned to look back at Clay, who trailed behind me in his Bigfoot form. "Just, don't shift until I tell them, okay? That way you can shift and change in my room. Call me selfish, I don't want anyone seeing you naked but me," I added with a half smile, trying to lighten the tension in the air. He nodded in agreement and kept pace with me as we headed towards the house. "I wonder why it's so quiet?" I remarked, noticing that no one had come out yet.

The silence was unsettling as we ascended the steps and onto the porch. Clay had positioned himself beside me. I pushed the door open and I called out for my sisters. "Ella? Theia? Anyone home?" My voice echoed in the stillness, met with silence, while Clay observed the surroundings suspiciously. My gaze landed on the coffee table, where there was a note pinned down with a knife. "Shift back," I told Clay as I approached the table, carefully tearing the note free from the grip of the hunting knife. I instantly recognized my sister's handwriting.

My eyes swept over the note, a shiver ran down my spine. My hands trembled as I passed it to Clay. "Clay-" I managed to utter, fear constricting my throat, "we have to find her before it's too late." A few centuries back, a pack of northern Werewolves and Lycans set out on a mission to eradicate Sirens. My sisters and I had narrowly escaped their

grasp— *until now.*

If you like paranormal romance then maybe you should check out The Coven Series by Dannie B.

For even more book recommendations check out my website:

https://ruthnalio.my.canva.site/dagf-ppve80

On my website you can find recaps of each of my books as they are published as well as hyperlinks to other books and some podcasts!

For bookish swag and signed physical copies of my books check out my etsy store:

https://www.etsy.com/shop/ruthnalio/?etsrc=sdt&fbclid=IwY2xjaw FKv6NleHRuA2FlbQIxMAABHSEeHDgJHCFpJG9maVxUTdwP Pb1Y_U4iNVlTDtbSDNJHMTDzC8ipw_f3lg_aem_B8FEtQ_vAFz Io_S7SGvsA

www.ingramcontent.com/pod-product-compliance
Lightning Source LLC
Chambersburg PA
CBHW031217260626
47169CB00007B/2092